Heal Me

ELLA JACOBS

ENSLAVED SERIES
BOOK THREE

HEAL ME

http://www.ellajacobs.com

Proofread by: The Blue Couch Edits

ISBN 978-87-975517-4-5

First Edition: May 2025

SHA-256 hash: eff8c6be56491aeb046e5218c

22a6ffdf56fe74f7432cefd2d3c399022fea41b

I used to have a voice.
A voice that would spellbind and enrapture.
I used to be someone.
Now I'm nothing.

Warning:
Pitch Black Darkness Ahead

Dear reader

This book *hurts.* There's no way around it. It's packed with heartbreak. But if you can hold on through the darkness, there'll be some light at the end.

It is pitch black, and especially the emotional content is heavy. If suicidal ideations and suicide attempts are a trigger for you, do not continue. This story contains many dark and potentially upsetting elements, so if you have any triggers at all, please check the full list on my website before diving in: ellajacobs.com.

Heal Me can be read as a standalone, but I recommend that you read *Take Me* and *Break Me* first. Although all three books are part of the same series, none of them are quite the same.

Please read responsibly.

Lots of dark love
Ella

1

LAVINIA

Tonight will be the last night I sing. The last night I get to share my voice with the world. The last night the world gets to hear my voice.

I'm going to miss this. Standing on a stage and pouring out my emotions to an audience that watches in silent awe. The crowded bar is unusually quiet tonight as I sing the wistful hymn of my home country that my mother used to sing to me. I think it's because they sense the unspoken—that I'm saying goodbye. In that potent act, I'm also reminiscing every wonderful and horrible memory.

The love and loss of my mother and sister. The hope my voice gave me, and the loss of innocence it caused. I sing for the ugly marks on my body that are constant reminders of the hell I went through when thinking luck had finally smiled upon me. But luck had nothing to do with the charming man who promised to take me away from these dingy bars and present me to the world. His smile was a hoax. A demon in disguise, luring in its prey.

He would have shown me fame and fortune if I had stayed with him. Of that I am sure. But the price was too high. Luck turned out to be a sick sadist with a knife who loved to cut into flesh. He crushed my hope and took me from my home country. A land corrupted and ugly, yet beautiful and magnificent in its own right. A place that offered my mother refuge when she fled from my father—the man who had offered her fields of gold. A man who came from the same country as the devil that lured me in.

The irony. Now I'm stuck here in Romania, without a penny to my name, unable to go home. I'm stuck wandering from one decrepit town to another, singing in these dingy bars, having lost everything I once held dear.

Everything except my voice and my face, which were too valuable for him to mar. No one wants to see an ugly woman sing, he always said. So he kept the ugliness restricted to places only he could see. And me. I see the ugliness each and every day. The scars covering my body. Red slices from where his knife broke my skin. Round burns from where he stubbed out his cigarettes.

A tear spills from my eye, and I realize the crowd has collectively lost its breath. I nearly lose my own. Because luck has finally turned my way. It has given me the exact end I wanted.

My eyes fall shut as I sing the last word. The last note I will ever sing. The room is dead still as the sound fades. No one moves; no one breathes. Not even me. The air buzzes with the intensity of emotion I've just instilled in each and every one of the men who has been listening attentively for the past hour.

This is a gift. Your ability to evoke such profound emotion, my mother used to say. Her words have never felt more true. I feel more connected to myself and the world around me, knowing I have left a piece of beauty among the barren brutality that pervades everywhere I go. I have given these people a glimpse of that hope I have always felt but have finally given up on.

I want to apologize for not giving them more of it. I want to promise to return. But I can't do that. I have to leave, just like the hope left me.

2

DORIN

The crowd is stunned. Struck silent by the angelic lilt of her voice, which lingers even after she's gone. A melody that will forever haunt them. No one has moved a finger or dared to draw a deep breath after she left the stage three minutes ago. I'm surprised to find I haven't either. She has woven her spell around me like she has everyone else.

Finally, the clapping starts. One person becomes two, two become four, and soon, the whole room is a loud din of constant noise. Clapping and cheering. Too many people. The noise dissolves the spell. Pollutes the beauty and casts the bar back into its sordid lowliness. Pathetic people, peeling paint, and a scent of grime so thick it sticks in my lungs the same way her song sticks in my mind, refusing to ever leave.

All the ugliness takes me back to my childhood. My father's nasty breath as he came home and woke me with a grip around my neck, yelling at me to get up and clean up the broken bottles.

With a jerk, I rise from the stool, badly needing to escape—the place, the crowd, and the memories. This is why I rarely leave the secluded peace of the castle in the Carpathian Mountains. It's the one place where I'm in control and the chaos of the world can't reach me.

Shoving at the cheering people, I jostle toward the exit and draw a heavy breath of fresh mountain air to cleanse the filth from my lungs. At least I didn't have to go to a polluted city to get this girl. If it had been anywhere else, I might have sent someone to get her, but I'm the one who found her, and she's my prize to claim. I heard her singing as I went into a bar, as shitty as the one I just left, to get a quick drink. I wanted to take her right then and there, but I already had a body in my trunk and didn't want to sully her with the foul blood of the slimy beast who thought he could cross me. When I came back for her the next day, she was gone, and I've been roaming these filthy towns for a week, searching for her.

I hide in the alley behind the bar, where I can watch both the rear exit and the front in case she dares to venture through the hungry crowd. Something tells me she won't do the latter. This girl was off the stage quicker than a mouse scurrying into its hole at the sight of an eagle descending from the sky. If I'm right, she'll be out in a few minutes, relieving me of the annoyance of having to wait.

Leaning back against a wall, I fiddle with the syringe in my pocket. As much as I like to hear them scream, I don't enjoy the hassle of getting a struggling girl out of a town, no matter how small. If she were any other girl, no one in this shitty town would care if I took her, but with this particular one, I'm thinking they'd have my head if they knew what I'm about to do. So I'm drugging her and saving the thrill of her screams for the seclusion of the dungeon—where I can do my thing in peace.

Five minutes pass, and I'm starting to wonder if I've read her wrong. But no. I easily recognized the look in her eyes as she cast a final glance at the crowd. That itchy eagerness to flee from everything and hide. I know it all too well myself.

Five more minutes and I'm getting really fucking irritated. I have done more than enough waiting in my life, and I'm not gonna stand around waiting for a girl one minute longer. Especially not one as eager to leave as her.

Stepping up to the back door, I carefully try the handle. It slides right open. It's almost too easy. I steal through a dark corridor, wincing as the vile smell once again infests my airways. At the end, I peer into a dimly lit backroom, expecting to find her there.

But it's empty. So I step into the room and look around—at the mirror above the table, where she must have sat before going on stage, the half-empty bottle of water she must have used to nurture her voice, and the tattered coat still hanging over the back of the wooden chair. Frowning, I step closer and notice the small purse on the table too. *She's still here?*

I scour the back area, checking the small toilet and a few closets without finding another trace of her. Then I unwillingly make my way back into the rowdy bar, do a round there, and go back as empty-handed as when I started.

Something's off. I feel it in my gut as I pick up her

bag and open it. Her wallet is sitting right there. It's like someone took her. Someone other than me. *Or maybe she ran,* I think as I notice the paper towel with black stains in the open bin. She did look utterly lost as she stopped singing. So lost, in fact, that I'm not surprised she would bolt without grabbing her things.

What the hell is going on with you, little songbird?

I grab her wallet and fish out her driver's license as I shove through the back entrance. Lavinia Corina Petrescu. Such a pretty name. It's almost a shame I'm replacing it with a number.

Her address is not far from here. I recognize the street name from when I passed through town on my way here. I get into my car at the side of the road and drive as fast as the weathered cobblestone will allow. Walking would be faster, but I need my car close by, so I can stuff her in the trunk as quickly as possible and go unnoticed.

The house I end up at has an orange façade as cracked as every other house in this miserable town, and the roof is crooked and falling apart. I cringe as another unwelcome memory of my childhood home assaults me. *At least she has a home,* I think as I approach the front door.

Or at least a roof over her head. Because this is not her house, I realize, as I see another name on the front door and notice her address has a B after the house number. Making my way to the back of the house, I find a back exit with the letter B on it. The door creaks way too loudly as I slide it open, and so do the stairs as I make my way up the moldy steps.

I stop before the weathered door that looks like it could barely keep out a racoon, considering how to proceed. Once I have the door open, I'll need to move quickly. If I'm guessing right, there's one room on the other side, and she'll see me the moment I enter. If I have to pick the lock, she might start screaming before I'm even in there, and I risk her subletters running up here, swinging a pitchfork at me. I'm not exactly in a mood to fight angry townsfolk tonight. I just want to grab the girl and get going. But it seems that's not an option, and I'm not sticking around here for a second longer than needed, so I grab the handle with a heavy sigh. Just like at the bar, it slides right open. And leaves me to stare into an empty room.

What the fuck. She's not here. Neither is anything else. An old mattress with a thin blanket, a lonely chair, and a small fridge. Her cell in the dungeon will barely be a downgrade. Once again, memories flash too vividly, making my steps too heavy, boots thudding against the floor as I go to the door that must lead to a bathroom. I'm almost tempted to go downstairs and beat the owner up for not providing better living quarters for this girl.

As I shove the door open, I am once again rendered stunned.

Nothing is going the way I planned it. Nothing I find is what I expect, and the sight that greets me is nearly too disturbing for me to take.

I have seen lots of blood in my life. Plenty of it. Red footprints when I stepped in glass. The taste of copper when my dad got mad. Streams of red spilling from *his* wounds when I got strong enough to fight back. Pools of blood gathering around shivering feet as screams sliced through the air and propelled me to strike again. I have beaten men to an inch of their lives and left them lying in a small sea of red. I have stitched up my own gaping wounds.

No, blood has never bothered me. Not until tonight.

Blood is supposed to be violent. Loud and chaotic. Full of hatred and agonizing despair. But the blood-red vision that meets me in this bathroom is none of that. It's quiet and thoughtful. Almost serene in some kind of warped way.

In an old, weathered bathtub sits the most beautiful creature I've ever encountered. Long, blonde tresses spill down milky white skin. Soft, plump lips tremble beneath the weight of what she's attempting. And wide green eyes stare down at the misplaced trail of red. So much red. It spills down the sides of both her wrists, into the water, enveloping this innocent beauty in a pool of red. But the morbidity doesn't end there. On the red water floats red leaves of rose petals, and candles on the sides of the tub flicker with a warm light more reminiscent of a romantic movie scene than a death ritual.

An angel in red.

Turning her head, she looks up at me and renders all my expectations useless for the hundredth time tonight. Her eyes are full of sorrow and defeat. Enough of it to end a life—but then again, not quite. As she speaks, those bright, blue orbs fill with a plea, almost like she wants me to finish the job for her.

"I can't do it," she says in a weak voice. "I can't do it," she repeats, shaking her head with utter defeat.

Sorrow makes her slump as she returns her attention to the knife in her hand and drags it across her wrist. More blood gushes from her, dripping down her milky skin.

I rush to her, but before I can grab the knife, she releases it herself, letting it plop into the water as a mournful sound escapes her. "I'm too weak," she whimpers as I grab her wrist to apply pressure to the wound. But there's no pulsing blood spurting from a major artery. The cut is superficial like every other stripe of red on her arms.

Burrowing her head into her blood-stained hands, she weeps. "I can't do it," she repeats over and over with aching defeat as I lift her out of the tub.

Sinking to the floor and settling her between my legs, I look around for something to bandage her cuts. They might not be deep enough to end her life immediately, but what she probably doesn't realize is that the amount of blood seeping from all those wounds will drain the life from her before long if I don't stop them. Her pulse is already weak as I press two fingers below her jaw.

I find nothing to aid me. Nothing but a dirty towel on the wall and a roll of toilet paper. So I rip my T-shirt off, cradling her against my chest with an arm around her waist as I tear it into strips. I'm surprised by the way she burrows into me, seeking comfort as she weeps. I don't stop to consider it—not her reaction or the way it makes me want to hold her and promise everything will be all right. Because it won't be if I don't do something about her wrists.

She keeps weeping into my shoulder, not protesting

the slightest as I grab one arm and wrap strips of fabric around the wounds, then do the same to the other. She has at least five cuts on each arm, but that isn't the worst. Old cuts and burns litter her skin, and once I've finished bandaging her arms and hold her before me, I notice the same marks on her torso.

I'm about to ask what happened—curiosity, I guess—but she has gone quiet, and I don't want to ruin whatever peace she's finally found. The weeping has stopped, and now she's only breathing a few staggered breaths and sniveling a bit as she hides her face in her bloody hands.

It's strange. No girl has ever calmed down in my presence. But this one seems to have found comfort in my arms, and some part of me wants to pull her back into me to see how it feels.

"Stay," I say as I get up.

She huddles around herself as I grab the towel and soak the tip in clean water from the sink. Then I sit beside her and start the long process of cleaning the blood from her body. It takes a while and several trips to the sink to wash the blood out of the towel. Still, not a single protest from her. Not even when I spread her legs to run the towel along the insides of her thighs.

Once I'm done, I help her up, all but lifting her as she struggles to find the strength to stand. I'm about to herd her out, sure she'll follow without question. This girl seems to have latched on to me, thinking I'm her savior or some shit like that. She doesn't even pull away as she finds her balance. She just keeps acting like I'm a goddamn rock for her to lean on, breathing shuddery sighs into her hands as she sinks into me.

I just stand there for a moment, watching her body tilt into mine as I consider my next step. The normal me would take the syringe in my pocket and stick it into her neck, haul her over my shoulder, and put her in the trunk of my car. But I guess this strange scenario must have gotten to me. Because what I do is nothing like anything I've ever done before. I scoop the girl into my arms, cradling her against my chest, and carefully turn to make sure I don't bump her head on the door frame as I leave the bathroom and the small room she calls home.

Instead of dumping her in the trunk, I open the back door and lay her on the backseat. Taking off my jacket, I use it as a makeshift blanket to cover her.

As I straighten, about to close the door, she looks at me again—the first time since I found her. Her lips part slightly as she whispers the strangest words a woman has ever spoken to me.

"Thank you."

3

LAVINIA

Everything is quiet. No rowdy men, rumbling cars, or rustling neighbors. No birds, no wind, no traffic in the distance.

Just quiet. And dark. Me and my own breaths.

It's peaceful. Like when I'm on stage and singing. That's the only time everything becomes truly quiet. The crowds go silent, and it's just me and my voice. I can close my eyes and pretend nothing else exists.

But once the hour is up and I've sung my full set, the world comes crashing back. People start clapping and whistling, and along with it comes memories of pain and fear. The struggle to get by. The struggle to escape. To find something better. To stay free. To stay alive.

There never is anything better, though. Freedom never feels free, alive never feels like living. It's always the same decrepit towns I end up in. Desperate people trying to get by, trying to find hope, or just trying to find whatever kick they can. My voice becomes a moment of escape for them, but once it's over, they go back to their usual ways. Foul words of derision when I ask for the full pay I was promised. Old ladies herding me out like vermin when I can't pay rent on time. Drunken men assaulting me in the back alleys behind the bars where they just adored me.

I can never stay long enough in one place to see if things will turn around if I get to know people. The risk of Zoltan finding me is too great, so I keep moving. On and on. Restlessly and relentlessly. All I can do is hope the next town will be better—that I'll somehow find a way out—but it's all the same. So I chose the only way out that was mine to choose.

Except, I couldn't find the courage to cut the knife deep enough.

Shame twists within me as I remember my pathetic attempts at cutting my wrists. It makes me feel more useless than anything else ever has.

Or maybe I did succeed after all, I think, as I stare into the black nothingness. Maybe I finally hit that artery and sank into darkness so quickly I can't remember it. Maybe I'm dead. Life is never this quiet. Never this dark.

I blink my eyes, turning my head a bit to try and catch sight of something. Everything remains pitch black. Unnaturally so.

Hope grows within me, but then I see a crack of light in the distance. It's small, but it's there. The darkness hasn't claimed me after all. But something else has, and despite it being dead still and confined, it brings me hope. Because it's something new. Something different. It doesn't look hopeful, but I've seen enough to know that looks can easily deceive. The home my mother built for my sister and me wasn't shiny and pretty, and when I did find something shiny and pretty, it was the den of the devil.

I search my brain to remember how I got here, but my head is blurry, and all I get are half-memories. Being lifted out of the tub. Crying into a strong shoulder. Falling asleep in the back of a car. I can't quite make sense of it; all I know is that none of it feels ominous. There was no threat, leery eyes, or violent hands. No charming smiles meant to deceive.

So I close my eyes and let the quietness engulf me.

* * *

Lights flickering on above me make me resurface to consciousness. A door creaks, and I turn on the mattress to see who's coming, blinking my eyes against the light as a tall, wide shadow appears through a door.

"Where am I?" I ask as the shadow approaches. Noticing I'm naked, I pull the thick blanket over me, and it's only then that I realize I'm not cold for the first time in forever. Blinking a little more, I see my surroundings and have my answer.

Four walls with white padding surround me. Even the door and the floor have the same cushion-like padding. The only surface left bare is the ceiling, which is bare, gray concrete.

Gulping, I turn my attention back to the gigantic man now towering above me.

"A mental facility," I whisper.

He doesn't confirm or refute. He just stands there, watching me for a minute.

It's the same man who found me in the tub when I

tried to take my life last night. He doesn't look like a doctor. There's nothing sophisticated, polished, or even composed about him as I'd expect from a doctor. This man looks brutal. Menacing, really. A scar slicing down the left side of his mouth bears witness to violence, and so does the hard stare of his dark eyes. His features are rough, his head bald, and his clothes consist of a simple black T-shirt, jeans, and boots. He's definitely not a doctor.

He has to be an orderly. It makes sense now that I think about it. His brawny build makes him perfect for handling belligerent patients. I cast another glance around the room and think to myself, *and throwing them into padded cells.*

What I don't understand is how he found me.

Pursing my lips, I shake my head as I try to find the right words. "Why… How? How did you know?"

"Know what?" He sinks to the floor beside the mattress, and I notice the bowl in his hand. Food. He's here to make sure I eat. Something I can barely manage myself these days—neither money-wise or energy-wise.

I gulp down a tight knot as I hold the blanket to my chest and scoot up to sit.

"How did you know I was…" I glance down at my arms and find white bandages instead of the black strips of his T-shirt. I don't even remember anyone changing those.

"I didn't," he says.

"Then why did you come? I mean, to my home."

"To bring you here."

"But if you didn't know, why would you come?"

Ignoring my question, he digs the spoon into the bowl and holds a large scoop of porridge to my mouth. I don't question him or think. I just open up and take it, feeling oddly grateful that someone would care enough to feed me. And not just feed me, but save my life too.

"Were you at the bar? Hearing me sing?" I ask before he holds another spoonful to my lips.

He meets my eyes again, and something flashes in his otherwise impassive expression. It's almost as if the memory haunts him. It's the same expression the crowd held as I sang for the last time—or I thought I did.

He doesn't say anything, but I think I know the answer. "Was it that obvious?" I ask. "That I was saying goodbye. Is that why you came? You had some kind of hunch or something?"

Once again, no reply. I take it as a yes, though. It's the only explanation that makes sense.

"How long are you keeping me here?" I ask.

"As long as—"

"No," I interrupt. "Don't answer. I don't want to know." I don't want to think about returning to the cruel world out there, where I don't belong and have nowhere to go. The thought of going back makes me want to rip those bandages right off and cut my arms anew. I want to stay in this quiet moment for as long as I can.

I open my mouth again when he holds the spoon to my lips. The porridge isn't half bad compared to the scraps I sometimes have to eat. It's actually sort of warm and hearty and reminds me of my mother making breakfast in our kitchen, back when I had a home. Back when I had *someone.*

It's only when the bowl is empty that I speak again. "What's your name?"

"Dorin," he says.

I give a slow nod and say quietly, "I'm Lavinia."

He just stares at me, not even acknowledging that he heard what I said. When he's about to get up, I hurriedly ask another question. "What's going to happen to me here?" I say, and when he stares off into the distance, seeming to consider my question, I add, "Some kind of therapy?"

He looks back at me, and there's a hint of a smile at the corners of his lips that I can't quite gauge. "Sure. Some kind of therapy."

4

DORIN

I'm more than confused as I leave the padded cell. I went in there thinking I'd feed her, then drag her out and start her training. But the way she reacted to me changed my motives. There was no fear or hatred in her eyes. She didn't think I was the devil or his spawn. She thought I was her savior. In a way, I guess I am, but if she knew what lies ahead, she wouldn't look at me with all that thankful vulnerability. She'd be screaming and cursing. I couldn't quite make myself ruin all that innocence yet. Plus, she seemed eager to believe she was in a mental facility, so it was easy enough to keep her in that illusion. I didn't even have to lie. All I needed was to stay quiet and let her come up with her own explanations. She even gave me the idea for my next step.

Some kind of therapy, she said.

I'm not going to bring her a doctor or a head shrink. The closest thing we have to a doctor is Dax and his medical training in the army, and the closest thing we have to the latter is Mikhail and his uncanny ability to read people. Neither will do her any good, and for some reason, I don't want either man to lay his hands on her or try to worm his way into her head.

What I can do is give her another type of therapy that will keep her in this ridiculous delusion for a while. I'm not sure why I want to feed the idea of this being a mental facility and not just tell her the truth. I'd do that with anyone else, if only just to see the horror on their face. Then I'd give them a good beating to welcome them and shove my cock into their ass while they were screaming.

But this girl has me doing everything differently. I didn't even give her the usual cold shower when I took her in last night. I just brought her straight to her cell, changed her bandages carefully, then left her to sleep.

I do have to do some things the usual way, though, or someone's bound to ask questions. If there's anything I hate, it's people sticking their noses in others' business. So I head for Dax's office. On my way there, I find a guard that I order to make sure to give her bathroom breaks since the padded cells don't have any toilets. Then I tell him the same as I tell every other guard and trainer I meet on the way: to keep their filthy hands off her and not say a single fucking word to her. This seems to be the new custom, after all—trainers getting to lay claim to girls. I fucking hated it when Mikhail did it with Nikolai's girl and the way Dax is doing it with this sub-training thing he has going. Right until this point.

"I need you to make a file on a new girl," I tell Dax once I'm in his office, sliding her driver's license across his desk where he's working on some leather project. His new sub is at his side, kneeling with her eyes downcast and hands placed on her thighs. If I didn't find this new training regime of his ridiculous, I'd be impressed by the way she just sits there, not even twitching a finger or chancing a glance up at my arrival.

"Sure." Dax grabs the license and flips his laptop open, and I watch his fingers tap away at the keys as he types in the information he has on her.

"What cell is she in?" he asks as he gets to the identification number, which indicates the year of arrival, how many girls came in before her said year, and her cell number.

"One," I say.

"One what?"

"Cell number zero one," I enunciate clearly as if he's dim-witted.

"Oh shit, Dorin, have you already messed her up that bad?"

The girls who end up in cell one, two, and three—the padded ones—usually don't go there before at least a few days, or, more likely, a few weeks. Most girls don't have the guts to try to end their own life, and insanity takes time. Even so, a pair of manacles can usually do the job. It's only when they start banging their heads against the concrete or damaging themselves in ways that decrease their value that we put them in there. Half the girls who go in there are beyond saving and end up in the incinerator room with my hands around their throats, writhing like beasts just before I snap their necks and throw them into the fire.

Ignoring his question, I say, "I need a paper bracelet instead of a chip."

He frowns at me but doesn't ask more questions.

This is one of the things I appreciate about Dax. He knows when to stay out of things and doesn't prod.

Dax types in more information and prints the bracelet. "All done," he says, handing it to me.

"Good. Tell everyone to keep their hands off her."

"Why?"

"None of your business," I clip and move to leave. Just as I'm about to shut the door behind me, I get an idea and pop my head back in. "Can I borrow your office tomorrow?"

"For what?"

"What do you think? For grooming my dog."

Dax sighs. "Just don't mess it all up. I don't want my walls covered in blood."

"I'll leave your office as clean as the queen's ass. Tomorrow. What time?"

He looks at his schedule on his desk. The man has a goddamn schedule as if he was some kind of actual doctor. Ridiculous.

"The day after tomorrow. One o'clock."

Perfect. At one o'clock in two days, my little songbird will receive her first therapy session.

* * *

As I leave Dax's office, I pass a whipping room with the door half ajar and a woman screaming bloody murder from the inside. Nothing unusual about the screaming, but we have a custom about keeping the doors closed—to maintain control and make sure no girl sees anything we don't want her to see—and something about the way she screams bugs me. I pop my head in to check what's going on. Like my stomach told me, I was right to. One of the new guards, Jan, has a girl suspended from the ceiling, so high only her toes are touching the floor, and ropes are cutting deep into her wrists. He's beating her with a heavy black cane, probably made of fiberglass. Everywhere. Even her ribs. Judging from the way she's breathing, I think he might have already cracked a few.

With four brisk steps, I cross the room and shove him aside.

"What the hell are you doing?" he barks.

"Stopping you from ruining the goods completely." Grabbing the ropes, I examine her hands and wrists. Her hands are blue to the point that it would be a miracle if she hasn't attained any nerve damage, and blood trickles from her wrists where the ropes dig so deep into her skin that I'm sure it will leave a scar.

I take my switchblade from my pocket and cut her loose, letting her crumple to the floor. Stepping over her, I unclip the baton on my belt. The heavy stick feels amazing in my hand. I loosen and tighten my fingers around the grip a few times, bouncing it lightly as I savor the sensation. This instrument is a good friend of mine that has been with me all the way. I got it from a cop that fucked over my former boss, before I came here. I took care of the traitor. He was my first kill on the job, and I've kept this lovely piece of reckoning as a souvenir. I've tried canes and whips, but I've never cared much for them. I like the weight of this stick in my hands too much.

I shove at Jan so hard he drops the cane. He crashes

back against the wall, and before he can recover, I slam the baton into his thighs. "How the hell is she supposed to give a good hand job with nerve damage?"

He pushes out from the wall and gives a foul sneer. "I'll just train her to give good blow jobs instead."

"That's not for you to decide." I swing the baton again, hard enough to send him back into the wall.

He growls and tries to snatch my baton, but a new blow to his thighs has his hands shooting down to protect the spot.

"It's not like you haven't done the fucking same," he accuses, biting back the pain as he straightens to face me head-on.

Prideful idiot. I shake my head. "And you think that gives you the right to do it?"

I swing the baton again, this time hitting his right upper arm—not hard enough to make any long-term damage, but enough that it's gonna hurt to swing the cane for a few days. "And don't strike their ribs. Fucking learn where to hit without damaging the goods." I make two quick swings, striking his round belly that provides more than enough cushioning to use as a target. "And learn some proper rope technique before tying up a girl again."

I reattach the baton to my belt and turn to leave.

There's a thud as he falls against the wall with a choked groan. "Fucking scarred-up freak," he calls out after me, his voice strained with the pain he tries to hide. "I'm sure your father enjoyed fucking you in the ass as a kid. Yeah, I've heard the stories."

It's tempting to go back and beat him some more,

but I don't have the time today, so I leave without granting him another look or warning. If this little beating didn't teach him the lesson he needed to learn, I'll gladly give him one that will.

5

LAVINIA

I spend most of the first two days here sleeping. I'm bone-tired, and this place has given me the peace I need to get some rest in my weary bones. Here, there's no stress of how to afford next week's rent, my next meal, or how to escape the men lurking in back alleys after a gig. I don't even have to fear Zoltan here. At least, so I think. Being shut in and isolated also means that everyone else is shut out.

The fact that I'm locked up doesn't even bother me. Freedom was always overrated. Nothing good ever came of it. Nothing but danger, loss, and uncertainty. The same goes for people. The isolation is blissful. I've always enjoyed being alone, and the world and all the people and noise in it have always seemed oppressive.

The first few times someone who's not Dorin comes in here, I'm on edge and nervous. They're all men, and none of them seem particularly friendly—which is to put it mildly. But none of them try to touch me or take advantage of my vulnerable state. They don't even speak to me, so I don't speak to them. They just bring me food, take me to the bathroom, or to a shower room where they hose me down with tepid water in the evenings.

It's not particularly comfortable. I'm always shivering after the showers, and the halls are barren, resembling an old dungeon more than a psychiatric facility. Once or twice, I even see an orderly drag a girl screaming down the hall. But then again, Romanian mental hospitals never did have a great reputation, and mental illness comes in many degrees and forms. All things considered, I guess this is better than what I could have feared. At least, I'm not in a crowded room with twenty others, the blankets in my cell keep me warm, and I get more food than I ever did beyond these walls.

As the shock and exhaustion wanes a bit on the second day, worry creeps in as I realize being locked up might not keep Zoltan out. He has more than enough money to bribe his way in, and this padded cell might be temporary. Once they deem me non-suicidal, they might move me to one of those crowded halls full of people, where it will be even easier for Zoltan to get to me.

I voice my concerns when Dorin brings me dinner. He's the only one who talks to me and the only one I feel comfortable talking to. *And* the only one who insists on feeding me. It's a bit unnerving, but I also feel oddly cared for when he brings the spoon to my mouth, providing me with the nourishment I always struggled to provide for myself.

"Can anyone get in here?" I ask a bit awkwardly halfway through the meal, fumbling with the blankets, unsure how to ask if my ex and stalker who caused all the ugly scars on my body can get to me here.

"What do you mean?"

"I mean... can anyone from the outside access me here?"

"No, this place is a fortress," he says, but I'm not sure he understands.

I usually don't tell anyone about Zoltan, afraid they'll want a ransom and take advantage of the situation, but there's nothing usual about this situation. And I feel a certain level of trust in this man. I'm not sure if it's a savior complex or if it's rational, and I'm not sure it matters. It's not like I have much of a choice, so I say, "Someone very rich is looking for me. I'm afraid he'll find me. I mean, now that I'm in the system."

"No one finds you here," he states, shoving another spoonful of beef stew toward my mouth.

I lean away from the spoon. "You don't know this man. He's dangerous. And rich. As in crazy amounts of money. If he bribes someone—"

Grabbing my jaw, he leans in close, watching me with a directness that has my breath stuttering. "No. One. Gets in here. I promise that."

I stare at him, baffled and unable to find any words. What he's saying isn't much of an assurance, but the way he says it...

"Do you understand?" he urges.

I nod in his hand.

"Now eat." He shoves the spoon back to my lips, forcing me to open promptly to avoid getting sauce down my chin. "You're too thin." A furrow forms between his brows as he throws a glance down my body, and I hug the blanket tighter.

"Can I get some clothes?" I ask him, just like I've

asked several of the other orderlies—or nurses, or whatever they are—without getting an answer.

"No clothes here."

"Why?"

He glances down my body again. "They get in the way."

I frown at this and bite my lips together. I don't like going naked. If all the orderlies had been women, I would've been okay, but they're all men. But then again, no one has tried anything—they barely even look at me—so I decide to let it go and inquire about something else instead.

"Are you gonna throw me into some crowded room once…" I shut my eyes and swallow hard.

"Once what?"

"Once I'm not suicidal anymore."

He swipes a gentle hand that seems too intimate to be professional over my cheek, and I open my eyes to stare into his deep brown ones as he says, "No. You'll stay here."

"Thank you," I whisper.

His head tilts slightly as if I've just said something weird, and he curves his palm around my cheek softly as he holds my gaze. "Tomorrow, you start therapy."

I nod. I don't know if it's supposed to be a reassurance or if it's just information. It doesn't matter. Right now, all I see is him and the comfort I find in the depths of his steady gaze.

* * *

Sometime after lunch the next day, Dorin comes to get me. I'm fidgeting and nervous as he walks me down the long, barren halls. I've never been in therapy, and the idea of dredging up all the hurt and grief that caused me to drag a knife across my wrists—and let it all out to a stranger—has my stomach churning.

"Can I at least get some clothes for this?" I can't open up like that when naked and vulnerable. There's no way.

"They'll get in the way," he says, repeating his vague answer from yesterday.

"What do you mean?" My voice goes up a pitch as he opens a door and herds me inside. What meets me in the room does nothing to alleviate the anxiety. Rather, it drives it through the roof. "What is this?" I squeal, backing up at the sight of a sort of exam table with restraints attached everywhere and stirrups where the lower half of the table is supposed to be.

"Get in," he says, pointing to the scary-looking chair.

"No." Hugging my arms around me, I back up another step. "You said therapy."

"Yes, therapy."

I shake my head, and my breaths go ragged as my back hits the wall.

"Electrotherapy," he clarifies.

"No!" How could I have thought I was safe here? I'm so desperate for safety that I'll take any resemblance of it I can get. But nothing in this world is safe. Yet, I keep grappling for it, because maybe—just maybe—this one time, I've gotten it all wrong.

"Are you at least gonna sedate me first?" I don't

know much about electrotherapy, but I do know that it has become a lot safer and more humane, and hope grows in me as I say the words.

Dorin smashes my hope as quickly as it came. “No.”

“What? No?” I push at him as he tries to grab my arm. “You can’t do this without sedation. It’s illegal. And you need a doctor for it. Will a doctor come?”

He grabs me under the arms, carries me flailing to the chair, and plops me into it. With a massive hand against my chest, he presses me down to half lie against the partially reclined seat. Wasting no time trying to calm me, he goes at the straps, pulling one over my chest and buckling it before moving on to draw one over my stomach. I throw my hands at the first one, fumbling at the buckle. With Dorin swatting my hands away, it takes a few tries, but I manage to open it and burst up to sit, grabbing the next strap.

With a grunt, Dorin snatches my wrist.

“Ah,” I cry at his terrifying grip that drains the strength from my arm, making my hand go slack. “You can’t do this,” I protest, shoving at his very big paws as he straps my hand to the side of the table.

“Why not?” he asks in an almost bored tone that scares me as much as his devastating strength.

The moment he releases my hand, I claw at the buckle to get it open, but before I can grab the strap, he has my other hand in an iron grip. I know I’ve lost as he leans over the table and forces my wrist into another strap, making me wince and whimper from the painful force.

“You can’t do this,” I repeat, defeat low lacing my

voice. "It's not legal." At least, I don't think it is. But psychiatric facilities are so underfunded and stigmatized in this country that I'm sure no one keeps track of what is going on in them. Especially not one as far away from civilization as this one must be. I have no idea where we are, but the village I was living in was as isolated as anything comes, and I have a hunch that Dorin hasn't taken me far. At least not far enough to reach any place meaningful.

Defeat becomes a heavy burden on my chest, pressing down and squeezing my lungs as I tug at my restrained hands without achieving anything. Pressing my head back into the chair, I stare at the ceiling, wishing I had been a little stronger. Wishing I could have found the strength to cut deep enough.

Dorin is quiet and methodical as he straps me down.

"Please," I implore in a weak voice as he lifts my feet into the stirrups. I have no idea why he needs my legs spread. All I can think is that this facility is far more corrupt than I could imagine. "Please don't do this. I'm not schizophrenic. Or depressed. This won't work on me."

He ignores my begging as he straps my legs in tight and proceeds to do the same with my hips, effectively displaying my private parts. It's not until he comes to stand by my head that I gain eye contact.

"You don't need to do this," I implore. "I'm already better. Just being here has helped. I'm not gonna take my own life."

Stroking his calloused palm over my head, he says, as if it's supposed to soothe me, "You don't have a choice."

Parting my lips, I shake my head as I try to find a response. But his words are so far out that there's nothing I can say. This place clearly works outside the bounds of reason, and nothing I say will change that.

"Now open your mouth." He picks something up from a side table, then smooths his hand over my forehead. Defeat is a sharp cut to my pride as I obey. It's the only thing I can do. Disobeying and having him force my mouth open would only cut even deeper.

He pushes a bite block between my teeth. A big one that fills out my mouth and forces it open. Then he uses roller gauze around my head and under my jaw to secure it in place. *There's nothing professional about this,* is all I can think as he winds the white material around my head. It's haphazard and makeshift. And it scares me to the bone.

Once he's done, he pulls a final strap over my forehead and steps to the other end of the table to take it all in.

With my mouth sealed shut, breathing through my nose becomes laborious as fear pulses faster through me. I struggle to look away as his eyes roam over me—my head and sealed mouth, my breasts and stomach, and my fully displayed pussy. I want to cry as his eyes go between my legs and pause there. But I refuse to give him my tears. I jerk against the straps instead, but all I manage is to flap my hands on the table and tap my heels against the stirrups.

Pulling up a rolling stool, Dorin takes a seat between my legs. My head is too far down to see what he's doing, but seeing his face is more than enough. A dark hue seems to settle over his expression as he drags a finger over my slit. But he doesn't stop there. He keeps going. Down to my ass, where he pauses right at my tight hole. As he turns his eyes to me, he reads all the fear and building panic in my wide eyes and shallow breaths. And he seems to feed on it. Tilting his head slightly, he watches me as if mesmerized as he presses. Just slightly. But enough to crank up my pulse further.

I whimper as he stretches my dry tissues. Little by little. Horror swirls in my brain as it dawns on me just where he's going to perform the electrotherapy, and panic closes in as I writhe against the straps, realizing just how little I can do about it.

Closing my eyes, I draw in on myself. No one has ever touched me there. Not even Zoltan. That's about the only pain he spared me. He wouldn't go anywhere near that filthy hole.

But now here I am, at a mental institution, having a stranger violating me *down there.* I want to scream and beg and fight, but there's nothing I can do. Nothing but getting caught in the riptide of my own panic.

A feral growl escapes him as he pushes in to the first knuckle. Forcing my eyes open, I stare at him, trying to plead with him through my gaze. If he goes any further without lubrication, he'll tear my skin.

He doesn't even look at me. All his attention is focused between my legs. All traces of care and gentleness have vanished in the blink of an eye. Something menacing has settled over his features, and it's only now that I notice how scary he actually is. I've been so caught up in the savior part of everything that I barely saw the scar, his gruff features, or his imposing build. But now, all I see is a sadistic beast.

His jaw tics and his finger jerks inside me. As he lets out another deep rumbling sound, I just know he's going to shove all the way in. I scream against the bite block to make him stop, but it's not my screams that have him pausing. It's the door opening and a bulky, long-haired man who comes in. He's not half as menacing as Dorin despite his muscular build and biker-like appearance, but more terrifying than most of the cruel men I've encountered, even so.

The new man pauses to watch the scene before him. The impassive, or maybe curious, expression on his face tells me he won't intervene even before he speaks.

"Electro play," he says, seeing the items on the rolling table. "Nice. Haven't done that in a while. Mind if I stay and watch?"

6

DORIN

"Get the fuck out of here," I snarl. Though, it's more of a habitual reaction to getting interrupted than anything else. As I cast a look at the girl on the table, I'm actually glad Dax came in and snapped me out of my sadistic tunnel vision. I was about to use her virgin ass. *Hard,* like I usually do. I have fucked enough women—and men—in the ass to know when it's a virgin hole, and I'd bet a million bucks this girl has never had a pinkie up there. Usually, that knowledge only drives me to go harder. I love to taint and tarnish innocent things. But all I see as I watch her milky white skin covered in cuts and burns is the broken woman in the bathtub. The one I saved.

I don't think I've ever saved a life before. I've taken plenty, but mercy has never been in my nature. With this girl, though, everything is different.

I've been going through my usual routines since I brought my little songbird to the dungeon—punishing women, fucking their assholes, and even branding one. But every time I step into her cell and see her petite frame and angelic face, something shifts inside me. Something that compels me to mend rather than break.

Possess rather than mar and discard.

Ignoring my rebuke, Dax points at the messy, but effective job I've done of keeping her quiet. "You know, I'm actually working on something that will do the job more efficiently. Something more convenient. Let me know if you'd like me to make a piece for you."

"This works fine," I tell him. It would be easier with something other than the gauze, but I kind of like the messy look. It's not that she even needs the protection for her teeth with the kind of electricity I'll be giving her, so I could have used a simple panel gag to shut her up, but that wouldn't play into her misconception of being at a mental facility.

Dax goes to grab something in a drawer across the room, and I can't help but notice how my little songbird stares after him with hopeful eyes. I'm sure that if her mouth wasn't stuffed and shut, she'd be begging Dax to get her out of this. She'd tell him how reckless I am for administering electrotherapy without a doctor present, that it's illegal without anesthesia, and how immoral it is to do it in the ass or some shit like that.

"What's so funny?" Dax asks as he passes me again.

"Nothing. I might tell you later." And maybe I will. Dax and I aren't close. I'm not close to anyone, really. But I guess he's the person whose company I tolerate the most down here. Once in a while, I even find it enjoyable. So maybe I'll let him in on this little game I'm playing with this girl. Or maybe not.

Once the door slams shut and we're alone again—just me and my quiet little victim—I go back to work. I never cover my hands, but once again, for the sake of the illusion, I break from my habits and snap on white latex gloves. Then I grab the long metal probe and smear lube on it before positioning it against her pussy. Only then do I look at her again. She's shuddering all over. Even her eyelids seem to tremble above her wide and unblinking eyes.

She can't see what's going on between her legs, but I made sure to move the probe through her line of sight to give her a good look at the polished metal.

She shakes her head against the leather strap as I push the tapered tip inside, and my dick strains against my jeans. The first violation is always the best. That initial terror combined with a sliver of hope that something just might shift. I relish every second of it, holding her gaze as I push it in.

A defeated whimper escapes her as I settle it deep inside her, and she shuts her eyes tight as the realization that she can't do shit washes over her. I finish with a wide strap that I draw between her legs and attach to the waist belt, keeping the probe locked in place.

Once the initial fear has waned, I don't care to draw things out anymore, so I grab the remote, set it at a medium voltage, and press the green button.

7

LAVINIA

Zap!

I cry out into the bite block as electricity jolts into my pussy. The sensation is horrible. Like getting slapped, but on the inside. Tears pool in my eyes, and breathing becomes almost impossible as I sniffle and hyperventilate at the same time.

Flapping my hands against the table, I try to signal for him to stop. *Not again! It's too much!* His eyes roam to my hands, and as if to prove just how little control I have, he presses the button again.

Zap!

I scream into the bite block as all my muscles go rigid. More tears form in my eyes, but I refuse to let them spill.

I can't breathe, I try to say, but the words die, breaking into a staggered sound as my stuffed mouth can't form them.

Zap!

More pain jolts into my nerves, making me spasm, the straps digging into my hips. The air in my lungs grows scarce as I draw shallow gasps through my stuffy nose. Black spots dance in my vision, and I know I'm going to faint if he zaps me again.

There's a rustling noise beside me. I vaguely notice that he's moving in the room, but my eyes are too blurry to tell what's happening.

Something presses against my face, and I strain against the leather strap to turn away from it.

"Breathe," a deep voice says above me. "This will help."

I pull in a staggered breath, and my lungs calm a little even though my nose is still stuffed and my breathing shallow. Repeating a few times, I find that the need for air eases, and I realize it's an oxygen mask he's holding to my face.

Relief is a small gust of wind that takes the edge of the panic. But nothing will make it go away entirely as I await the next jolt of electricity. I tense against the straps, blinking my moist eyes up at my tormentor as I try to gauge when he'll press the button again.

His expression is closed off and unreadable as he stares back at me, taking in every nuance of desperation and terror written across my face. He just stands there for a while, watching me, before he loosens the head strap to pull the elastic band on the mask over my head. With the mask in place, he buckles the strap again and returns to sit between my legs.

I keep panting, feeling devastatingly helpless, unable to move an inch, unable to form a single protest. Not even with Zoltan did I ever feel this powerless. He would always let me fight him and allow me enough leeway to at least try and pull away from the lashes of his belt when he tied me up. I even got to choose between the horrors he inflicted upon me sometimes. But here, the powerlessness cuts particularly deep.

When Dorin removes the wide strap that keeps the probe in place, my breathing calms somewhat at the prospect of him removing it. Deep down, I know it's not over yet—if he was done, he wouldn't have fastened the mask—but I need to believe, if only just for a few seconds, to calm the violent beating of my heart.

A new wave of horror crashes over me when he presses the rubbery end of a long device to my clit. A magic wand. The same type of vibrator Zoltan used to push me close to the peak repeatedly, only to stop the moment I was about to go over. It was a special kind of torture, sometimes even worse than his knife. He'd keep going for hours, leaving my body hollow and weak, yet forcing it through another strenuous rise toward an orgasm, only to end it in a hard crash.

I want to demand to know what he's doing. This is a psychiatric facility. He can't use me sexually. He just can't. If I told his superior, he'd get fired.

I want to scream this at him, but part of me knows how ridiculous it would be.

His boss is probably as immoral as him. The man who came in here earlier didn't bat an eye at the scene unfolding before him. He even saw Dorin poke a finger into my ass. No, I'm fucked. I'm truly trapped now. With Zoltan, I always had the choice to run away, but here, there's no escape.

Zap!

I convulse against the straps as a current of

electricity stronger than the previous slams against my inner walls. A scream tears from my throat as my eyes roll back. The pain is numbing, and I think it's going to knock me out. But then the vibrations start, and a new sort of sensation awakens my body, forcing me to stay conscious.

I try to fight it. The same way I did so many times with Zoltan. But just like then, there's no ignoring the pulsing sensations thrumming against my sensitive clit and rippling through my core. I've always reacted strongly to this kind of stimuli, and this man is going to take advantage of it just like Zoltan did.

Mournful whimpers form in my throat. It's all so hopeless. My body awakens, slowly but surely, humming with the need for sweet release that I know I'm not going to get. My whimpers turn into moans, and soon, I'm bucking into the straps for a whole different reason.

Something simmers in my tormentor's eyes. I'm not sure what it is. Triumph, power, maybe lust. The sick bastard enjoys this. Even so, I try to beg him through my eyes—to not zap me again, to let me come, or remove the vibrator before I'm close.

Shame clenches my chest as pleasure twists and twirls at my core, dragging me dangerously close to the edge. I shut my eyes to hide as I fail to suppress a loud moan. I brace for the disappointment—or maybe relief—of him cutting off my orgasm. But he never does. He lets me fall over the edge. But just as I moan my release into the bite block, a zap jolts against my insides.

I cry out as pain tears through my core, but it's not as violent as before. It's like the pleasure cushions the blow, and as the jerky sensations recede, I realize I'm as needy as before. The vibrations keep pulsing against my clit, and with the remaining sensations of the electric current still humming at my core, I crash straight toward another orgasm.

Zap!

This time, the jolt doesn't cut off my orgasm. Rather, it seems to feed it. I come apart in a burst of sensation as painful as it's ecstatic. Fireworks explode in my brain as I moan and groan, scream and wail into the block. It's too much. I spasm against the straps, almost cramping everywhere.

When I blink my heavy eyelids open, my vision is swimming, but I can clearly make out the wide smirk on Dorin's face. Part of me wants to smile back because I just experienced the greatest ecstasy of my life. Another part of me wants to curse him for taking advantage of my vulnerability and finding enjoyment in my torment.

Being too weak to do either, I let my eyes fall shut again.

But Dorin isn't finished. Far from it. He takes my body through four more rounds of ecstatic pleasure and painful torment. Once he removes the probe and starts unbuckling the straps, my body is weak and covered in a slick coat of sweat, and I'm barely even cognizant. Yet I don't feel exhausted in that bone-deep achy way as when Zoltan was finished with me for the night. This is a floatier kind of sensation as if I've just been freed from the strain and stress of my body—or finally found release from all those denied orgasms.

It doesn't make sense, and I don't think further about it as Dorin carries me out of the room.

8

LAVINIA

I must have fallen asleep because when I wake up, I'm on the mattress in my cell, and someone is washing me with a warm cloth. The calm motions are soothing, and I keep my eyes closed for a while. My body doesn't seem to want to wake up anyway. My limbs are sluggish in a calm sort of way, and my brain seems to have turned off. Post-orgasmic bliss.

Warm, big hands lift my arms and legs, turn me onto my stomach and back again as they wash me. They seem strong and capable. Protective even.

As I slowly come to and memories rush in—the zaps, the helplessness, and the violations—I force my eyes open and pull away from the big hands.

"Uh-uh," someone scolds. My savior and tormentor. The man who took me from my pathetic existence and saved me from myself. But also the man who violated my body.

And made me feel this deep-seated peace.

No, what he did was wrong.

Pushing up to sit, I lean against the wall and direct my sleepy eyes at him. "Why did you do that?"

"What?" he asks, dipping the terry cloth in a bucket of water.

I lift my shoulders. "Everything." Shame clogs my throat as I try to put voice to the things he did.

"The electrotherapy?" he asks, taking my arm from where I'm hugging my waist. When I try to pull it back, he simply tightens his grip. It's not punishing, but firm enough to let me know I have no say.

"Everything," I repeat. "Touching me like that. Making me—" I gulp against the thick knot in my throat. "Making me come."

"It's the way we do things around here."

Tears well in my eyes—they seem to be doing that a lot since he found me and I wept in his arms. I bite my lips to hide the tremor that threatens to pull me under. I watch my arm as he moves the gray cloth over my pale skin. The bandages are gone, and the vision that remains is a disturbing but familiar one. Angry red cuts slash across my milky skin, and a new well of shame crashes over me and makes me huddle in the corner. *I did that.*

I try to close my eyes, but my mind refuses to let me forget. It assaults me with memories of the blood spilling into the clear water, tainting it and surrounding me in the kind of violence I badly wanted to escape. So I open my eyes again and try to focus on something else. His hands. They are big and strong with prominent veins that bulge beneath olive-toned skin. Moving my eyes up, I watch his arm, the thick layer of hair covering his skin, and the strong muscles that bulge as he dips the cloth in the bucket and wrings it. As I watch closely, I notice marks beneath the layer of hairs. Scars. Scars that are very similar to mine. Thin cuts and round blotches.

I don't realize what I'm doing before my fingers graze his skin and he jerks his arm away.

"I'm sorry," I say, drawing my hand back.

He watches me warily for a moment, the faint lines on his forehead deepening and his whole stance tightening. But as our eyes interlock, something changes in his expression. His eyes roam down my body, the many scars and burns marring my skin the same way it does his.

His taut expression slowly softens, and he moves his arm back to grab the cloth he dropped in the bucket. He stares down at the dripping water as he wrings the cloth anew. "It's okay. You can touch them."

My breath shudders past my lips as I reach out and graze one of the scars. He stiffens for a second, and I pause, hovering right above the old cut, just barely touching him.

"What happened?" I whisper.

"A knife," he simply says, taking my other arm to continue washing even though he's already cleaned that one.

"Whose knife?"

He sighs and closes his eyes, opens them back up, and faces me with a look that seems to hold a world of hurt. "My dad's."

Words fail me as I imagine a little boy getting cut and burned by the person they should trust the most in the world. When I finally do speak, the words seem ridiculous, but it's all my brain can think to say. "Did he smoke?" I ask as I move my fingers to one of the round protrusions on his skin.

He nods as he watches the mark I'm hovering at.

Looking down at my stomach and the round scars there, I say in a low voice, "So did Zoltan."

An angry growl startles me, making me look up and see a flicker of something feral pass over Dorin's features just before he grabs my jaw and leans so close I can't see anything but his eyes. In a deep, firm voice, he says, as if it's a promise more important than the very air he breathes, "I'll kill him."

My breath sticks in my throat. I have no idea what to say. His words are abrupt and absurd, coming out of nowhere. Yet they're somehow the best words I've ever heard. Words of protection that no one has ever come close to matching.

I say the only thing that makes sense in this warped moment of intimacy. "Thank you."

He keeps the silent connection for a moment, branding his promise into me with a burning stare that reduces my defenses to ashes. He's still right in front of me as he says, "Sing for me." It's not a question, not a command. It's just the way things have to be.

I don't think, I just open my mouth and sing. A gentle, sorrowful folk tune my mother used to sing for me. Besides loosening his grip on my jaw to let my mouth form the words, he stays where he is, a breath away from my lips, enclosing us in our own private world, caught in a strange sort of intimacy that seems wholly unfamiliar yet completely right.

When the last word has left my lips, he hovers a moment longer. Then he lets out a pleased hum, grabs my waist, and pulls me down to lie on the mattress.

I think he's going to take advantage and fuck me. I even think I'll let him. But he simply tucks me in, grabs the bucket, and leaves.

For a long time after he's gone, I just lie there, staring at the door, trying to figure out what's happened. When all the mixed signals and strange events only leave my head in tangles, I stop thinking altogether and drift off.

9

DORIN

The static chaos in my head that always haunts me is unusually quiet as I leave my songbird's cell. The noises, the memories, and the derisive castigations are all gone. It's unnerving. The screams of others are usually the only thing that will drown them out, but her singing did it too—and not just drown them out but chase them away.

What disturbs me even more is that I told her about my scars. I even let her touch them. I've never told anyone how I got them. Many people have asked, but they only do so once, quickly realizing it's a bad fucking idea. But with this girl, I felt no need to shut her up or even intimidate her into doing so. Instead, I gave her an answer.

Why the hell would I do that? Vulnerability is weakness, and I'm not the one who's weak here.

Anger simmers to life inside me, and as I pass a guard, I set down the bucket and fix him with a glare that has the usual almost-pissing-his-pants effect. "Clean this up. And go bandage the arms of the girl in cell one. But don't speak a single fucking word to her or we're gonna have a problem." I don't bother standing around to see if the idiot got the message; I know he did. He was there the last time someone disobeyed me.

Then I veer down the corridor that holds most of the normal cells and open a random one. I need to clear my mind.

"Get up," I demand, and the girl scrambles to get off the mattress. With her arms shackled to the wall, she doesn't get far.

"I-I'm sorry, sir," she stutters.

I slap her across the face. "Learn to speak right or don't speak at all."

She falls against the wall, screeching as she scrapes her bare skin against the rough surface. She scrambles to get up on her knees again, but I'm impatient. I don't care where or how I do this; I just need to do it.

Grabbing her hips, I flip her around and place her on all fours. "Don't move a fucking muscle," I tell her as I unclip my stick from my belt and relish the heavy weight in my hand. I hate how I've been leaving it in the hall every time I go into cell one, to avoid ruining the illusion of a mental facility. I don't even know why I'm playing into it. I should just get it over with, let her know where she is, let her feel my stick against her skin and my cock in her ass.

But as I imagine that it's her frail body in front of me—her blonde locks spilling down her milky skin and the many scars marring the perfect beauty, yet somehow enhancing it—I feel sick to my stomach at what I'm about to do. So I grab a handful of the girl's straight, black hair to remind myself that she isn't the little songbird as I swing my stick against her ass. Her flesh is already bruised, but I don't care about those marks like I do the scars and bruises on *her.*

Her scream is a welcome noise to fill my head again. The silence was eerie. I swing my stick to hear it again. Over and over until only faint whimpers remain and her head is hanging by my grip in her hair.

"Fucking bitch." I yank her ass back up as she's about to collapse on the mattress, part her ass cheeks, and spit on her tight hole—the opening that's nowhere near as tight and inviting as my songbird's virgin asshole.

"Fuck," I growl, ignoring the girl's pathetic begging as I force my hard dick inside her. I need to get the blonde girl out of my head. But as I ram into the black-haired bitch, the little songbird keeps popping into my mind. I imagine her muffled screams as I zapped her. Her desperate straining against the straps. But most of all, I imagine her sweet little moans as I forced her to come. Her pretty voice as she sang to me.

"Get out of my fucking head," I growl as my balls start to draw up. But she won't leave, so I flip the girl over and stand with my feet on each side of her. "Open your mouth," I bark with a bite that has her obeying immediately.

Her eyes fill with fear and disgust as I jerk off, aiming my cock directly at her mouth.

"That's right, I just had it in your ass, and now my cum is getting in your mouth. I hope you can taste it."

She whimpers pathetically but keeps her mouth open anyway as I spurt my release into and around her mouth. But there's not much satisfaction to be found. Not even when I crouch over her and force her to lick my cock clean.

"Useless whore," I spit, finishing off with a kick to her side before leaving. Then I ignore the urge to go back to my little songbird to hear her sing and retreat to my chambers upstairs instead. My dog, Rex, and a long run in the woods is the next best thing when I'm on edge and the girls don't cut it.

Rex yaps happily as I enter my quarters, jumping up and giving me a wet lick on the cheek.

"You know I hate that shit," I tell him. Yet I've never trained the big German shepherd to quit it. He can do many tricks and will obey everything else in an instant, but I never had the heart to wean him off that bad habit.

I make quick work of changing into sweatpants, then open the door and wave at Rex. "Come on. Let's go run this shit off."

10

LAVINIA

When Dorin comes to my cell with a bowl of breakfast the next day, I have gained some more perspective and realized just how fucked up everything that happened yesterday is. It's just a matter of time before Dorin will take advantage of the situation and force himself upon me, and I have to do whatever I can to prevent it.

"I want to see the doctor in charge," I say, sitting up straight to feel more assertive.

He doesn't even answer as he comes to stand before me.

I try not to let his intimidating size and terrifyingly cold gaze deter me, but keeping my spine straight beneath him is impossible as I speak again. "I'll tell someone what you did."

He lifts a brow and huffs, but I refuse to give up this easily.

"You can't do this, it's il—"

"It's illegal?" he cuts me off. "Immoral, wrong, and all that shit. Is that what you're gonna say?"

Gulping, I nod.

His jaw ticks as he crouches in front of me, sets the

bowl on the floor, and grabs my chin. "You might not like the kind of therapy we offer here, but it's the only fucking one you're getting."

"I don't want it. I never consented to any of this."

"Do you really think your consent matters?"

"I don't care, just let me out of here."

"Do you?" he demands, raising his voice as he digs his fingers into my jaw.

"Yes. I mean. No," I blurt, and fuck, that last word hurts. Because, of course, it doesn't. He gained the right to override my consent the moment I slit my wrists and became a danger to myself. "But that doesn't give you the right to do whatever you want. It's not right what you did yesterday."

Leaning closer, he says, "Like I told you, that's the way we do things around here." Then he releases me.

But I'm not half done. "I want to speak to your supervisor."

Ignoring my stubbornness, he scoops up a spoonful of porridge and holds it to my mouth. "Eat."

"Not until you let me talk to someone in charge."

Grabbing the top of my head with his huge hand, he holds me in place as he presses the spoon to my mouth, smearing porridge onto my lips as I refuse to part them. His cruel force is so humiliating that I throw up my hands and push at his arm, making the spoon fly to the side, porridge spattering over the padded floor.

"Goddammit," he growls and snatches my wrist in a bruising grip.

"Ouch, you're hurting me," I squeal, clawing at his fingers.

He simply grabs my other hand too and gathers them in one big hand that easily encompasses both my slender wrists. I struggle to get free, but it's useless as he lowers my arms toward the mattress, twisting them into an awkward angle that hurts at the slightest movement.

Using his free hand, he takes his phone from his pocket and calls someone. "Get me a straitjacket," he orders. The person on the line asks something, and Dorin answers, "Number one." He's about to put the phone down, but adds, "*And* all the gear to go along with it."

"Let me go," I beg as we wait. "You're hurting me."

Dorin is unyielding, keeping me in the strained position until an orderly comes rushing with a pile of things that he sets on the floor beside Dorin before scurrying off again. The way he keeps his eyes averted and hurries off makes me think he's afraid of Dorin. But before I can process the notion, Dorin has my right arm stretched out, shoving it into a white sleeve. A new sort of urgency drives me into a frenzy as my fingers end up in a closed sleeve. *A straitjacket.*

"No!" I yell, refusing to take this humiliation. The full brunt of being at a mental facility is finally catching up to me. I might have attempted suicide, but I'm not crazy. I'm not so out of my mind that I'd bang my head against the wall or claw at my own skin. They don't need to keep me in a padded cell. They don't need to give me fucked-up electrotherapy, and they certainly don't need to put me in a straitjacket.

Tugging at my arm, I try to pull out of the sleeve, but Dorin is strong. Terrifyingly so. I'm a mouse caught in the claws of a lion as he forces my left arm into the other sleeve. Within seconds, he has the thing on me and shoves me to my stomach. Humiliation unlike any I've ever experienced claws at my insides as I flail without gaining anything.

With a knee on my back, he easily closes the buckles. I try to claw and grab at him, but the closed sleeves and my trapped position render my fight utterly pathetic, and I feel like I'm actually going crazy as I start to scream.

"Stop! You can't do this! I have rights!"

He hoists me up on my knees, and I writhe and jerk as he pulls my arms through the vertical strap at the front, then shoves me back onto my stomach and buckles the sleeves on the back.

Tears pool in my eyes as I tug at my arms, only to meet the tight resistance of the trapped sleeves. With each pull, I sink deeper into the humiliation until I barely feel like a person. Yet I can't stop fighting. Because it's the only thing that keeps my last sliver of dignity intact.

"Open your mouth," Dorin says, pressing a hand to my back to keep me still as he holds something in front of my face.

As I see a black rubber ball on a leather strap, everything inside me freezes. I go still, barely breathing, as I watch the thing. "No, please," I finally manage. "I'll be quiet. I'll be still."

"Open. Your. Mouth." His voice lowers to a raspy growl, more beast than human, and terror is an icy bucket of water that freezes my resistance.

Squeezing my eyes shut, I part my lips.

Shoving his fingers into my mouth, he pries it

farther open and pushes the ball inside. Tears leak from my eyes as he pulls the straps around my head and buckles them together, locking the ball in place between my teeth.

I'm not the type of person who cries a lot. I learned to stay strong for my baby sister when our mother got sick and I had to earn enough money to keep us in our house and keep us fed, and I've learned to do things that tore my pride to shreds when I lost both my mother, sister, and our home in one cruel twist of fate. I've begged in the streets and I've sold my body without shedding a single tear. Not even Zoltan, with his cutting knife and burning cigarettes, could draw more than a few drops from my eyes. I wouldn't allow it. But somehow, the things this man does to me are worse than any other. His humiliations cut deeper than a knife on my skin. It sears into the very core of my being, tears me open, and breaks me apart. Zoltan violated my body, but this man violates my soul.

And he's not even done yet; he picks up another item and pushes my legs apart. I want to fight—close my legs and kick at him. But I can't. My limbs are paralyzed as I lie there, reduced to an animal with no rights.

The tears come faster as he prods something smooth at my pussy. Finding my opening dry, he moves the thing back, and the *pfft* sound as he spits only drives the humiliation deeper. I weep as he prods the now wet item at my opening, jerking as he shoves it—the head of a dildo—inside. Clenching my inner muscles, I try to block further advance, but as he moves it back and forth a few times, my muscles loosen, and he slides it in. Slowly, the wide thing drags along my inner walls, awakening unwanted sensations in my sensitive folds even as the dildo scratches at my dry walls.

Dorin hums as he pushes the thing in place. "This will make you feel better." He grabs the bottom strap on the front of the jacket, pulls it between my legs, and straps it on the back, effectively keeping the dildo in place.

The remaining crumbs of my resistance disintegrate in a flood of defeat. My tears soak the mattress, and spit drips from my mouth around the gag as I lose myself to utter grief.

Dorin carefully moves me onto my back and positions me as comfortably as possible. I close my eyes tight as he strokes the hair from my face and wipes at the tears and drool on my cheeks.

"This will help," he says in a gentle tone as if he truly believes it.

I shake my head, but the movement is feeble.

"Look at me," he urges softly, stroking my cheek with the back of his wide hand. When I don't respond, he repeats, "Look at me, little songbird."

I let my eyes fall open, and meeting the brown depths of Dorin's gaze is startling. They hold an almost compassionate expression that slips straight past my tattered defenses to nestle at the very root of my starved being.

"Such a pretty songbird," he says. No further degradation or smearing my helplessness in my face. His words are gentle and honest. It's more than I can take. More than I can resist. Giving in to a bone-deep grief, I lean into his hand and weep, seeking comfort from the same man who broke me.

"This will help," he repeats, pressing a button on a small remote in his other hand.

My eyes widen as the dildo comes alive with soft vibrations. Vibrations that are like sweet caresses on my insides.

"Just give in to it," he coaxes as he keeps caressing my skin. "It will all feel better if you do. I promise."

With all logic and reason crushed under a heavy load of defeat, there's nothing left for me to fight off his words with. Not even the will to resist. Because I badly need something—anything—to mend this broken feeling inside. So I give in to the humming vibrations and nod as I fall captive to the soft promise in his eyes.

I sniffle and swallow repeatedly to try and control myself, but there's nothing I can do. Spit keeps dripping from my mouth, and soon, snot slips from my nose too.

"It's okay," he says, turning his hand to curve his warm palm around the side of my face. "Just give in. I've got you." He presses the button again, turning the vibrations up higher.

I press my head into his hand and close my eyes as tingling sensations erupt at my core, awakening my tired body and humming in my nerves.

Turning the vibrations up another notch, he puts the remote away to curve his other hand around my face too. Warmth engulfs me as his enormous hands cover both sides of my face. It's comfort and protection. Affection and care. I soak it up like a starved cat as I sink into the sensations. The heat, the humming, and the heaviness in my body. I let it sweep me away to another world. A place where dignity, hopes, and dreams don't matter. It's light and freeing—to let go of everything that has always burdened and disappointed me. To open up and let this man take it all away—take everything away to give me this. I'm not even sure what it is, and it doesn't matter as tingling sensations pulse at my core and sweep through my body while his steady presence engulfs me and takes away the pain.

The sensations swirl and expand as the dildo keeps vibrating against my sensitive core. Liquid heat gathers around it, and my muscles soften and contract as my whole body seems to pulse along with it. Moans form behind the gag, mixing with my whimpers as I cry. The crying doesn't feel as strained anymore. It's no longer a burden.

It's freeing.

My back arches as heat coalesces deep within my belly, and I strain against the straitjacket. Even the tight constriction is no longer oppressive.

"I've got you. I'm right here. Just let go," Dorin says, and as I push my arms against the tight sleeves again, it's more like a warm hug than a cruel humiliation. It sends a wave of energy straight to my core, making my toes curl, and when I repeat the motion, I come apart.

Sweet relief washes through me in a wave of heat. I moan. Long and deep. A freeing sound from the pit of my belly.

"Look at me," Dorin says.

As I open my eyes and stare up at this stranger who has reached deeper inside me than anyone else, I feel new. Cleansed.

11

DORIN

Her eyes are swimming and unfocused, her limbs loose and heavy, as I help her up to sit. Having to support her to keep her upright, I scoot onto the mattress and nestle her into my side as I unbuckle the gag. Her small, pliant body feels surprisingly good against mine, so instead of placing her against the wall, I keep her at my side as I lift the bowl of kasha to feed her.

All thoughts seem to have vanished from her mind, leaving her in a floaty, almost drugged state. I'm not sure she even realizes what's going on as she opens her mouth to accept the food. It seems to be a reflexive response. One that I enjoy more than I would have thought. I have always found willing obedience overrated and never did understand Mikhail's and Dax's fascination with Nikolai's submissive girl—and now, Dax's little project. But something about this girl makes me appreciate things I've never cared for before. It's as unsettling as it is fascinating.

Little by little, she regains awareness. Her head moves more as she accepts each scoop and chews, and she stirs to get more comfortable against my side. But even after she has eaten the last spoonful of kasha, she remains quiet and still.

I let her sit there for a few minutes, curious to see what she'll do. When she shows no signs of change, I lower her to the mattress and cover her with the blankets, then get up to leave to give her some time to rest. When I open the door, there's a small mewl, maybe half a word, that makes me turn. Her eyes are now focused on me, though just barely, and her lips move as she struggles to put voice to her words.

"Stay."

I'm barely sure I heard right. Her voice is so weak that the word is almost intelligible, and the idea of a girl wanting me to stay is laughable, but the pleading look in her eyes tells me she does indeed mean it.

Pausing, I consider if I want to stay and am surprised to find that I do. So I return to sit on the mattress beside her. No touching, just sitting there.

My presence seems to calm her. She closes her eyes, and her breaths deepen as relief seems to wash through her.

I lean against the wall and carefully press my palm to her forehead. I half expect her to pull away like a scared cat, but she only hums. It's a soft, low sound, barely there, but as I start stroking her skin, she repeats, and peace seems to settle over her.

I'm not sure how long I stay there, just sitting at her side, stroking her hair. When I catch myself nodding off for the second time, I decide it's time to leave.

She's fast asleep, breathing calmly. She only stirs a little as I remove the dildo, but falls back to sleep immediately again. I'm about to turn her to remove the straitjacket but change my mind as I watch the peaceful expression on her face. Such a different look than the one I found her with in the tub. I don't want to ruin that, so I decide to come back later.

Besides, I like having her helpless here, waiting for me.

As I leave her cell and walk away, I grit my teeth at the sound of a voice these halls have been blissfully void of for the better part of several months.

"What the hell is going on here?" Mikhail calls out, making me stop and turn. He's been gone on business, as he often is, and as always, I'm not exactly happy to have him back. I prefer to be my own boss and not have some annoying prick in a fancy suit breathing down my neck about money and profits and not damaging the merchandise. "You're supposed to keep an eye on things when I'm gone," he continues, stopping in front of me—closer than anyone else dares to. "Now I have four barely sellable girls. One girl because Dax can't do his job and hands it over to you, and three others because the new guy, Jan, is out of control. And everyone keeps whispering about the girl in cell one. Explain."

"I told you that fucker was up to no good when you hired him," I shoot back, having had a bad feeling about Jan from the start. Mikhail surely knew even before I told him but chose to ignore his instincts, badly needing more trainers.

"I need you to put him in line. But no killing him. I need him back in shape in two weeks."

"Sure," I say in a non-committed tone and begin to

walk away.

Grabbing my arm to make me turn, Mikhail gets himself goddamn close to getting my fist in his face. "I'm serious, Dorin. I'm getting a new shipment, and I won't have the manpower to train them if we're a man down."

"Two weeks, and you make sure no one touches *her.*" I stab my finger through the air toward the cell I just left.

"She's all yours as long as you keep your end of the deal."

Without another word, I walk away to go find Jan. He's in the middle of beating up a girl in one of the whipping rooms. I can tell from her shallow breaths and hunched-forward posture that he has already broken one of her ribs. He's about to break another as he lifts his fist, aiming for her chest.

Goddamn idiot. I told him not to hit their ribs, and now he's taking it one step further, breaking them.

Shaking my head, I cross the room and punch his face with enough force to send him to the ground. Then I cut the ropes on the girl's wrists and carry her into the hallway, where I dump her on the ground. Someone else will take her away when they find her.

Stepping back into the room, I expect an attack as the guy tries to retaliate, but he just lies there. Leaning down over him, I press my fingers to his pulse point and find a steady beat. *Good,* he's just out for a minute. I was looking forward to this, so it would be a great disappointment if I had accidentally killed him. I always do enjoy the aftermath of beating up one of the trainers, seeing the way the others cower when I pass them in the halls. The few strikes with my baton weren't enough to have that effect on Jan, but I'll make sure to remedy that today.

Taking a seat on the chair in the corner, I wait.

It takes longer than expected for him to wake up, but I don't mind. The humming anticipation in my body is almost as good as the beating itself. My cock is already twitching in my pants.

Popping the top button on my jeans, I decide to give it some attention to pass the time. I wrap my hand around it and stroke gently as I imagine my fist connecting with flesh again and again. My eyes fall shut as I imagine beating the guy to the ground and towering over him as he lies there whimpering.

At some point, my train of thought shifts. New images mix with the violent ones of blood spilling and bones snapping. My little songbird appears before my inner eye. Trapped in the straitjacket and at my mercy. Eyes lost and vulnerable as she whimpers around the gag. Moans forming in her throat as she fails to resist the pleasure I force upon her.

I groan as my dick swells and my balls draw up. I pick up speed, stroking harder, slowing down again as I'm about to come. I want to save my orgasm for when Jan wakes up. So I keep going like that for a while, pumping my cock until I'm close to the edge, then slowing down to languid strokes.

I'm close to the peak when something moves before me. I open my eyes to see the small, pudgy man come barging at me, fist raised in the air and eyes full of fury. I lean to the side just in time to avoid his fist breaking my nose. Slamming my hand onto his throat, I throw him forward. He falls to the ground and slides two feet across the floor, groaning from the rough landing.

He's not giving up, though. I have only just buttoned my pants and pushed to my feet when he charges again.

I shake my head at his predictability. His fist is already in the air and aimed. There's no element of surprise. *What an amateur.* Just as he thinks he's going to get me, I lift my own fist and shove it into his gut. I barely need to put in any force since he has done all the work for me, coming running full speed and slamming himself onto it.

He doubles over but throws a punch anyway. It's uncoordinated and sloppy. I don't even need to sidestep. I kick his legs out from under him and wait for him to crawl to his knees before I deliver the next kick. It takes six more punches and kicks before he stays down. Then I deliver a few more, making sure not to break any important bones. I only break his nose to get back at him for him trying to break mine. Once I deem him on the verge of consciousness, I sink onto my knees behind him, pull him up on all fours, and hold him there as I take out my knife. Slipping the blade under the hem of his pants, I cut them open to reveal his ass crack. It's hairy and ugly as fuck, but I don't care. Parting the cheeks, I spit on his tight opening, and that's when it seems to dawn on him what I'm about to do.

The realization sends a new burst of adrenaline through him, and he struggles like a squealing pig as I press my hard cock against his opening. But he can't escape my vise-like grip on his hips, and no ass is too tight. Eventually, I always get in. It takes a few minutes of more spitting, prodding with my fingers, and hauling him back into position when I release him to use my hands.

Finally, I have the tip inside and am advancing. His walls clench me tight as though he's milking me and not trying to push me out, and I shove his head to the ground to let the hard stone swallow his pathetic screams as I start moving in and out. Fucking heaven, a tight virgin ass like this. I close my eyes, and there she is again. My sweet songbird. I wish it was her ass and not some pathetic idiot as I pick up pace and my balls start to draw up.

The orgasm is disappointing, to say the least. I try to imagine her soft skin, but all I feel is the coarse hairs on this prick's rough skin. He squeals and screams as I shoot my load inside him. It's annoying as hell, and I deliver a few more kicks to his side to punish him for it before I leave to go wash the blood off my dick.

12

LAVINIA

A few days of quiet routine, time passing in a sort of mindless haze, is all I get before Dorin announces the next violation.

"Time for therapy," he says in a clipped voice as he comes into my cell sometime after feeding me the second bowl of porridge of the day.

"You don't need to do this," I protest, but my voice is weak as I lift my hand to dry the tears gathering in my eyes. Since the episode with the straitjacket a few days ago, it's been a constant battle to keep them at bay, and my fight has drained wholly and utterly. I spend hours upon hours sleeping, and whenever Dorin comes into my cell, I meekly follow his instructions, opening my mouth to let him feed me and now getting off the mattress to let him take me to get electrotherapy. I don't know why. Part of me thinks I've fallen into a deep depression, but as he closes his strong fingers around my arm, I feel this urgent pull that begs me to sink into him and seek that same comfort he gave me after he'd shattered my dignity—and set me free.

I want to feel that again. Badly. But as he leads me down the hall, all I can think about is the terrifying pain of the electrotherapy.

I'm trembling, my legs threatening to give in, once he opens the door to the medical room.

"Please," I try one more time in a weak voice at the sight of the horrifying chair with the stirrups and all the straps.

"This will help you," he insists, spurring me on with a small push at my back.

I scoot onto the chair, not knowing what else to do. It's all so very hopeless.

Dorin straps me in tight like the last time. Arms, legs, chest, stomach. So many straps I can barely count. A tight knot keeps growing in my throat to the point where I can barely breathe. I feel faint and nauseous by the time he grabs the bite block from the side table.

"Open your mouth," he says.

"I don't feel so good," I tell him weakly.

His impassive gaze roams over my face, and the harshness of his features seems to soften somewhat as he watches me. A line forms between his brows, and it almost looks like worry. He pushes the bite block in place, nonetheless, when I slacken my jaw and part my lips.

Next comes the thick layers of roller gauze to keep my mouth shut and the bite block in place.

I squeeze my eyes closed to block everything out. Defeat is a heavy weight on my chest as Dorin presses my head into the seat and pulls a final strap over my forehead.

At that moment of searing helplessness, there's only one thought in my mind. Regret. Deep, aching regret.

I should have sliced the knife deeper.

13

DORIN

An unfamiliar sense of worry gnaws at me as I take a seat between her legs and lift the butt plug connected to the power box, smearing it with lube. Her eyes are shut tight, her limbs trembling, and her skin is pale—not just milky white, but sickly so. And she hasn't even realized which hole I intend to use yet.

I've been hell-bent on using her ass since I fucked Jan and all I could think about was sinking into her tight opening. I waited a couple of days, seeing how she seemed exhausted and needing time to process, but today, I couldn't wait any longer. I woke up with a raging hard-on and the sound of her helpless mewls stuck on repeat in my mind. It's only because I jerked off twice—once in the shower and once on a girl I'd just punished—that it's the plug and not my cock going inside her tight opening. I don't want to break her and make her bleed like I do with most girls down here, and something compels me to keep her in this crazy mental facility illusion for a while longer, so this is how I'll do it. I'll train her ass slowly with the pretense of giving her electrotherapy, and my cock will have to wait.

But as I'm about to push the plug against her narrow opening and glance up, I pause. For the same reasons—which I can't quite fathom—that I don't want to break her ass, I don't want to break *her.* Something tells me that's exactly what I'll be doing if I proceed like this.

I put away the butt plug, grab the vibrator wand instead, and smear it with lube.

A terrified yelp escapes her as I press it to the top of her pussy, and she clenches her fists with a strength that has her knuckles turning as white as her face.

"No electricity yet," I reassure. "I'll prepare you a bit first, so it won't be as painful."

She yelps as I press the button to start the vibrations, and her eyes fly open—wide, terrified, and confused. But also relieved after a few seconds as my words seem to register.

I keep the vibrations at a low setting, not wanting to draw out her need too quickly and make her desperate for release. She's not getting an orgasm before I've done what I came here for—at least the electro part of it.

Slowly, the color returns to her face as blood seeps into her cheeks, creating a nice rosy hue, and the tension drains from her fisted hands, her hips moving in tiny wriggles against the leather belts.

When she lets out a tiny moan behind the thick layer of gauze, I know she's ready.

I put the vibrator aside and pick up the probe for her pussy. Her eyes widen as she watches me smear lube onto it, but her breaths remain lustful pants, and her hips keep moving ever so slightly.

As I grab the remote control, I consider starting at a

low voltage, but I've already shown her more than plenty of mercy. I set it at a high medium and press the button.

A surge of power rushes through me as she jerks, squeezing her eyes shut and crying out into the bite block. But along with the rush comes that unfamiliar worry again as I wait to see her reaction.

Fuck, if it isn't the best thing I've ever seen as she watches me with wide eyes full of utter vulnerability. The fear and pain are still there, but so is acceptance. There's nothing she can do about this, but instead of fighting it, she accepts it and lets me take control.

So I do just that. I turn the voltage up, just a smidgen, and press the button again. Her wail has my cock straining against my pants, and I trail my eyes over her body in fascination as her muscles coil tight, then slowly relax. Her eyes peel open, swimming with worry and desire, and this time, a few tears.

One spills over and trails down her cheek, and it causes her to squeeze her eyes shut, trying to rein them in. To hide from me.

A surge of anger twitches in my fingers, and I turn the voltage up a decent notch and zap her. *I won't have her hiding from me.*

This time, her scream is hysteric, and her eyes remain shut as she jerks and strains. Tears spill down the sides of her face, and her jaw tightens as she bites her teeth together—the same thing she does whenever she tries to hide and hold back the grief. She clenches it so tight I can see it even behind the thick layer of gauze.

"Look at me," I say, but she shakes her head against the head strap, and her refusal sends a surge of irate energy through my blood.

"Look at me," I demand with a power that bounces off the walls and makes her eyes fly open. Pushing up from the stool, I'm at her side in a flash, claiming those eyes before she can shut them again. Pressing a hand on the opposite side of the table, I lean down to make my eyes the only goddamn thing she sees. Because that's what I want. I want to be the only thing that matters to her. I want to consume her world, draw out her pain, and coax her desire. In that warped moment, I want it fucking all.

"Don't you dare close your eyes again," I say with a rumbling warning.

More tears flow down her cheeks, and her chest shakes with ragged breaths as she struggles to hold in the grief and the shock.

But I won't let her. Grabbing her chin, I demand her full attention as I press the button again.

She cries out into the makeshift gag, convulsing hard as the pain zaps through her.

"Look at me," I demand the moment her eyes snap shut.

She obeys. It's the sweetest goddamn thing I've ever seen as she peels her eyes open and stares up at me with a deep plea in her eyes, her brows tightening with barely processed pain and grief, and tears welling and spilling.

"So fucking beautiful," I say, leaning down to press my lips to her forehead, below the strap.

Confusion flickers in her wide eyes as I draw back, just enough to see those eyes. "Give me those tears, pretty songbird. I want to see you cry." I put down the remote, release the head strap, and press my hand to her cheek. "Give me all that pain and grief, so I can take it away."

She gives the slightest shake of her head, but the tears are already coming faster, her breaths shaking with suppressed sobs. Her jaw clenches and unclenches, and her fists do the same as a world of pain seems to rise and fall within her. She's holding back, but also trying to release it.

She's still thinking too much, so I take the remote again, turn up the voltage, and press.

Even muffled by the stuffing in her mouth, her scream is shrill and painful as she bucks her strung-tight body against the restraints. It's almost painful to witness, but powerful, nonetheless.

Before she can disappear into herself, I press my forehead to hers and whisper, "Stay with me."

I have no idea what I'm doing. For a moment as I stand there, cupping her cheeks and holding her with an intimacy I've never understood, I see myself from the outside. It feels pathetic, and I'm about to pull away. But then her eyes draw open, and a sob wrenches from her chest, setting loose a cascade of tears that spills onto my hands in warm splashes of sorrowful rain.

All thoughts vanish as she becomes the only thing that matters—keeping her safe and taking away her pain.

"Let it loose, my little songbird," I urge. "I've got you. I'll keep you safe."

More sobs rack through her body, making her shake against the leather, and her breathing becomes hazardous above the gauze as she struggles to draw in air through her nose. Her despair is so deep it aches in my own heart, breathing life into the cold and quiet organ that I shut down so many years ago when I was just a boy.

It's not for her sake that I suddenly have my knife out to cut loose the gauze, then unbuckle the straps with hastened motions. *It's for me.*

The moment the last strap is gone, I hoist her up. A relief unlike any I've ever felt washes over me as I sit on the edge of the padded surface and curl her into my arms. Her hands clutch my T-shirt with a desperation that seems to ache in her very bones, and grief sends ugly sounds up through her chest as she presses her head into my shoulder. But there's nothing ugly about her. Her pain is the most beautiful, raw, and honest thing I've ever felt, and I relish every second of it as I hold her tight.

"I've got you. No one's going to hurt you as long as I have you," I promise. It just might be the sincerest words I've ever spoken.

14

LAVINIA

I scream with the full force of my lungs as the knife cuts along the flesh on my stomach.

Zoltan's eyes are wide and protruding, like a demon clawing through the flesh of its victim, as he watches the blood trickle out of the wound.

I can't see it myself—I don't dare to look down there again. The last time I did, I nearly fainted at the sight of red smeared across the whole area.

But Zoltan refuses to let me forget. He drags his sweaty palm over my stomach. It's like salt in the many wounds. But what's worse is when he lifts that same hand to my face. I want to shut my eyes, but I'm frozen in place, staring at that blood-red hand coming for me.

I scream again as he drags it over my face, finally managing to shut my eyes.

The scent of copper fills my senses, drawing a wave of nausea up my throat. I swallow repeatedly to suppress it.

"It's a shame I can't use the knife here," he drawls, pressing the side of the knife to my cheek. I lie deadly still, barely daring to breathe as he leans in, his stale breath blowing hard against my skin right above the blade. "No

one would pay to see a cut-up whore sing now, would they?"

He presses his pelvis into me, rubbing his hard cock along my slit. Keeping the knife where it is, he reaches down to smear his dick in my blood, using it as lube before he shoves it into my dry opening.

I squeeze my eyes shut as the raw sensation tears through my tissues, squeezing my jaw tight as I suppress the heavy well of grief and despair at losing myself—my dignity and my worth. I don't dare to move the tiniest bit as he keeps the knife pressed to my cheek. I just lie there, letting him fuck me, hating myself for staying.

"Stop," I croak in a weak voice.

He pauses inside me. "If I stop, you won't get to sing."

I hold my breath as I weigh my options. If I tell him to stop, he'll throw me back into the streets, where strangers will rape and abuse me—where I'm nothing and no one. If I let him continue, he'll tear through my dignity and drag me through more agony. My dignity is not worth much as is, but on the streets, my worthlessness will be on full display. With Zoltan, I can keep it hidden. He wraps me in pretty clothes and shows me off to fancy people, spares my pretty face and promises to let the world hear me sing.

He promises to let me have the one thing left that truly matters to me. My voice. *He'll let me share it with the world and everyone in it. Just one more day with him, and I'll get to sing on the big stage he has booked. I'll finally get to soar.*

So I stay quiet, and he starts moving again.

As Zoltan fucks me, I fill my mind with images of a red curtain going up, me standing on that stage, singing my heart out, and the audience struck into silence as they watch and absorb the deep-felt emotions I can only pour out through my voice. I imagine my song moving them the same way my music did my mother and sister—being the only comfort I could offer when times were bleak.

I will sing for them—*finally fulfill my purpose, bringing solace to the world with my voice, like my mother would say.*

But the images can only keep me from reality for so long. Tears start pressing behind my eyes at the thought of the only two people I ever truly loved—the ones who were cruelly ripped away from me. My tears are the one thing I won't let Zoltan have. It's the only part of my dignity I can save.

So I drift back to the present. The stabbing thrusts in my pelvis, the devil hiding behind a charming smile, and the searing pain in the cuts on my stomach. I bite down on my jaw and muster all my will. Because I won't cry for him.

But Zoltan is not done trying as he comes inside me and pulls out. He wants everything, *and he's determined to take my tears.*

As if reading my thoughts, he says, "Stubborn bitch. You really think you can keep those tears from me?"

I don't give him an answer. I don't react until he moves the blade back to my torso—to my ribs.

"Let's see if the blade slicing across bone will do the trick." He gives me a cruel smile, eyes widening with sadistic insanity, nostrils flaring with beastly lust.

"Don't," I say in a hoarse voice as I stare up at him. "Zoltan, please don't."

"That's right, beg me, bitch. And then cry." He drags the knife across my skin, digging deep, slicing across my raw bones.

Agony unlike any I've ever known screeches in my nerves, flaying my mind and crushing me into pieces. Nails on a chalkboard, a fork on a plate. The pain even seems to ring in my ears. It closes up my throat, snuffing shut my voice and my lungs.

For a moment, I just lie there, frozen into place, mouth slightly ajar as I stare emptily at the ceiling.

"Cry," he demands.

Finally, I manage a word. "Stop," I choke out in a hoarse voice. If he keeps going like this, I won't be able to sing tomorrow—before all those people he has gathered to make me into a star.

"Then cry," he snarls, moving the knife to the next rib and slicing through my flesh.

The pain explodes—in my mind, my body, and my every sense. It cuts through everything I am and was. My hopes, my dreams, and the final scraps of worth I've been clinging to. That final cut makes everything clear, just before it steals my consciousness and thrusts me into pitch-black blissful darkness.

* * *

I wake up drenched in cold sweat, my heart pounding like it's about to give in.

A deep pain aches in my body, but I can't tell if it's real or a memory.

I open my eyes but don't see anything. For a

moment, I think this is it. *Zoltan killed me.*

But then I inspect my surroundings with my hands—the foam mattress, the rough blankets, and the padded walls.

I'm not with Zoltan.

Or maybe I am?

Maybe he's lurking in the deep shadows, ready to jump?

Steps echo through the hall outside my cell. Maybe that's him, finally having found me and bribed his way in?

Or maybe he's been here all along, having paid someone to lock me up in here, taking his time to torment me before he pounces himself?

Or maybe he has brought me out of that facility, locked me in some new padded cell he has made for me at his estate.

There's no way to tell.

My mind spirals out of control, paranoid and wild.

I push up to sit, staring into the darkness, searching for some kind of reassurance. There's none to find.

My heart beats faster and faster. My airways narrow as the darkness closes tight around me. I feel like I'm choking.

"Please," I wheeze, pressing my hands to my tight chest. "Is anyone there?" I move to crawl across the floor, trying to raise my voice as I go. "Help me. Please, I can't breathe." I can't muster much strength between my heaving breaths, so I take to knocking at the door instead. Tiny slaps at the padding turn to pounding fists as my desperation rises.

"Get me out of here," I croak as panic threatens to snuff me out—the same way Zoltan's knife did. "Please." I bang harder as I hear steps in the hall. "Help me."

There's a tiny beep, and the door flies open.

I scramble back as a tall figure towers above me. I can't make him out. I can't see if it's *him*, and suddenly, I want the door closed again.

"What the fuck's your problem," the man bites. "Get back to bed and stay quiet."

It's not Zoltan's voice, but the knowledge offers no relief. I'm stuck in the spiraling panic, my breaths stuck at the top of my throat. "I ca-can't breathe."

Another tall shape appears before me, and the two start talking.

"It's Dorin's bitch. She was banging on the door, panicking. Should we call Dorin?"

"In the middle of the night and wake him up? He'll have our asses. Just leave her be."

"And what do you think he'll do if she chokes to death?"

"You can't die from a panic attack," one of them says with ridicule.

"I don't know. I'm not risking anything. Have you seen the way Dorin acts around her?"

I don't register the meaning of their words. They get sucked straight into the chaos of my mind, feeding the whirlwind that blinds me to the world around me. All I see is Zoltan's blood-red hands; all I feel is that blade slicing across my ribs. The lingering fear that he's close keeps pulsing in my heart until a dizzy sensation threatens to take me out.

15

DORIN

It's three in the morning when I wake from my phone buzzing.

"What?" I snap as I answer the call.

"Um, it's that girl you keep in cell one. I'm sorry to wake you, it's just—"

"What is it with her?" Having a bad feeling, I'm already out of bed, pulling on my jeans with one hand as I try to get a sensible explanation out of the idiot on guard duty tonight. "Did someone touch her?"

"No!" he all but gasps. "We didn't lay a hand on her, I swear."

"Then tell me what the hell's going on."

"She's panicking, says she can't breathe. I think she's about to pass out."

"You'd better make sure she doesn't," I snap and hang up, hurrying out of the bedroom.

Rex is already at the front door, wide awake and alert with his tail wagging and tongue sticking out of his mouth, watching me eagerly as I stick my feet into my boots.

"Sorry, buddy," I say, giving him a pat on the head.

"It's not time for our morning run yet."

Leaving him behind, I rush down the seven flights of stairs, cursing myself for having picked the rooms in the tower—isolated and undisturbed, but as far away from my little songbird as I can get.

My heart is hammering against my rib cage once I reach her cell. Not because of exertion but because I'm goddamned scared.

I'm about to bark at the two guards and demand to know what happened. But when I see the fragile girl huddled in the corner, head pressed between her knees as she hyperventilates, I flip straight from punish-mode to another mode far less violent but equally urgent.

"Get the fuck out of here," I demand, rushing into the cell and pulling the shaking girl into my arms. "Get me something hot to drink," I call out after them.

One of the idiots sticks his head back in. "What?"

"Something hot to drink," I enunciate with a sharp edge. "And some chocolate."

He gives me a confused look but hurries off, nonetheless—hopefully to do what I said if he knows what's good for him.

"Breathe in through your nose and hold it for a few seconds," I tell her, remembering how my old boss used to handle his daughter's panic attacks back when I was a bodyguard for a Russian mobster many years ago. She draws in a shuddery breath, but I can tell it's superficial, and the air goes straight back out. "Uh-uh, deeper."

"I can't," she whimpers, trying and failing again.

I turn her around, grabbing her arms as I seek out eye contact. "Look at me," I demand, feeling a bit panicked myself when she shakes her head and keeps her eyes down.

"Look at me," I try again with the bite that usually makes everyone obey. It doesn't help. If anything, she seems to curl more in on herself.

I take a deep breath myself, then wrap my hands around the sides of her head and lean in close. "Look at me," I repeat, this time in a long, deep voice.

Her eyes flicker up and away. It's not much, but it's an improvement.

"Good. Do that again and now keep your eyes on me."

Her blue orbs are full of desperation, her brows knitted together as she finally lifts her gaze to mine and keeps it there.

"That's it. Now breathe. In through your nose." I draw in a deep breath through my nose, and a small smile plays at my lips when she follows. "Now hold it." Her chest shudders, but she manages to hold it anyway until I say, "And breathe out."

Her breath gushes out, and then she's hyperventilating again. I make her repeat the in-through-your-nose-out-through-your-mouth technique, and slowly, her breaths calm. A strange sensation warms my chest as she sits there, watching me with big round eyes, breaths coming in shuddery, but slow drags. I think it might be pride—in her for doing it and maybe a little in myself for making her do it. It's a strange sensation. One I don't get to linger on as the guard returns.

"I'm really sorry I woke you up," he says, voice strained, as he comes in and places a small tray with a steaming cup of tea and a bowl of chocolate beside us.

"Just shut up and get out," I whisper to not cause my songbird any further shock. "And close the door," I add. I want to be alone with her. And she needs to feel safe.

"Is he here? Has he found me?" she asks in a weak voice, turning her head to look frantically around her as the door closes.

"No one's here. It's just me," I assure her.

"But is he *here?*"

"Who?"

"Zoltan."

Of course. She's talking about the man who hurt her. The man who cut her up and stubbed out cigarettes on her skin. The man I'm itching to kill each and every time I look at the many scars he left on her body. I promised her I'd kill him, and I fully intend to do so. Right now, though, I'm too caught up here, making sure none of the idiots touch my songbird, to go chase down some rich bastard. If he's as powerful as she suggested, he'll be easy enough to find once I do decide to go looking for him, and I'll make sure to make his death extra painful to compensate for the extra time I'm giving him.

I capture her head between my hands again. "Zoltan is not here. You're safe. I'll protect you. No one's gonna touch you here. No one but me. Do you see how those men cowered and fled?"

She gives a slight shake of her head, then seems to remember and nods.

"They'll do whatever I say. You're safe here. You're under my protection."

I pull her close, and the feeling as she burrows into

me calms my pounding heart that I didn't even realize was still hammering.

"I'll protect you," I say, and the sincerity I put into those words takes me aback. I don't know what it is about this girl, but she brings out new sides of me—sides I've never encountered before. As I feed her chocolate and tea, I only find it growing, making me want to stay. I ease us both onto the mattress and nestle her into me, just lying there with her for a while, enjoying the calm feeling of her slow breaths as she sinks into me and finds peace.

"What happened?" I finally inquire. I'm about to ask if any of the men touched her but stop myself, remembering that I have an illusion to maintain. What's already happened tonight has probably done plenty to make her question it.

"Nightmare," she says, tension seeping back into her muscles.

"Was it Zoltan?"

She gives a slow nod as a shuddery breath passes through her lips.

"What did he do?"

I've never cared to listen to anyone for long, but as my little songbird tells me about her dream, I find myself wanting to know it all. I ask about her life, how she met Zoltan, and how she got away. I listen attentively as she tells me how she lost her mother and her sister in a fire, which burned down her childhood home and everything she ever held dear, while she was out, trying to earn enough money to keep said home. I listen as she tells me how she struggled to get by on the streets, all alone. How

Zoltan found her singing at a bar, took her from homeless poverty, and promised to give her a better life, then gave her hell. Anger boils inside me as she tells me how he gradually ramped up the abuse and how she finally ran off after she'd passed out from the pain, realizing that the next time, or the time after that, she might not wake up again.

"That night was a year before you found me. To the date." She gives a humorless laugh. "I spent a year going from place to place, living off what little I could earn from singing, hoping I could find something—anything—for me out there. All I found was more misery, only in new shapes and forms. I decided to give it a year. If nothing got better, I would take control over my own life and end it on my own terms." She makes a shuddery sigh. "But I guess I wasn't strong enough."

I prop myself up on my elbow, gently turning her to lie on her back. "You know what I thought when I found you?"

"No."

"I found you so brave for making that decision."

"Brave? I couldn't even cut deep enough."

"You still made the decision, to go there. I never could do that. I was always weak like that."

"Weak? How could you even say that?" She lifts her hand, touching her slender fingers to my face. The gesture is startling, and I nearly pull away. But as she curves her hand around my cheek, the warmth of her palm connecting with my skin, I lift my own hand, covering hers to keep it there. "There's nothing weak about you." She looks back and forth between my eyes. "I believe you when you say you'll protect me. There's no one else I'd feel safer hearing those words from."

My pulse speeds up as I stare at her, utterly mesmerized by her beauty, her words, her vulnerability, and the strength that shines through despite her brokenness. I want to absorb her so I can be close to that strength all the time. I want to absorb her utterly and completely, but I'm afraid I will taint her beauty and lose it for good. Things always have a way of withering and wilting close to me.

At that moment, I decide that I'll do everything in my power to make sure that doesn't happen to my sweet songbird. I don't know how, so that's something I'll have to figure out. For now, I'll go easy on her, and instead of trying to get closer, I remain where I am and ask her to give me the one thing she can give without risking me ruining it.

"Sing to me."

16

LAVINIA

Things sort of stagnate after the nightmare and the night I spent with Dorin, opening up my heart to him, in both spoken and sung words.

He seems to grow even more protective of me, coming to my cell several times a day, taking me to get showered himself, and asking me how I'm feeling. At the same time, I feel like he's distancing himself. He'll touch me to give me comfort, but he doesn't take me to get electrotherapy again or do any other inappropriate things to me.

I should be happy about this development, but part of me misses it—the way he made me forget everything. The way he made me feel cleansed and new. As if he somehow reset my mind with the warped things he did.

I ask him a few times when I'll get to see a doctor or get some real treatment, but he always evades my questions or answers vaguely.

It makes me wonder about this place—if it really is what he says it is. Maybe they don't care about treatment at all? Maybe they just care about getting the insane people off the streets—away from everyone else? Maybe this is just a prison disguised as a mental facility? And maybe I'll spend the rest of my life in this cell?

Or maybe it's something entirely different.

I always shudder at that last thought and try to reason that it really is a mental facility. But it's difficult. There are too many things pointing in other directions. Such as the strange way the men seemed to fear Dorin when I had the nightmare. I try to chalk it up to part of the illicitness of this place—that there's some kind of hierarchy between the orderlies. And maybe the place is even more corrupt than it appears—there's more abuse going on than I thought. Maybe what I'm experiencing is nothing compared to what others endure. Maybe I'm lucky to have Dorin taken his liking to me. If he hadn't done that, maybe the other men would use me in even worse ways.

Or maybe it isn't a mental facility at all.

All these thoughts rush through my mind as the days drag on, making me feel like I'm going insane.

I can't figure out if I'm paranoid, if something worse than a little corruption really is amiss here, or if it's the isolation that's *making* me insane. To avoid the latter, I start singing to myself. It's the only thing I can do here. I sing all the songs my mother taught me, all the ones I've picked up in the various places I've been, and I even come up with new ones myself.

But not even singing will chase away this new unease creeping along the edges of my mind. I need answers, so I decide to try to get some from Dorin.

"What's going to happen to me?" I ask him one morning when he brings me breakfast. "Please tell me; I need to know."

"Your situation is being evaluated," he says, vague as always.

"By who? Shouldn't I see a doctor? No one's been here to evaluate me."

"That's not for you to worry about." He sits on the mattress, pulls me between his legs, and scoops a big spoonful of yogurt and fresh fruit up, holding it to my lips. He's been feeding me different things lately—more flavorful and varied food. It helps a bit to have my senses awakened like that, but it's far from enough to cut through the stagnant, dead routine I'm stuck in.

I push his hand away and turn to look at the closed door. "Please, Dorin. I'm going insane, just sitting here all day, all alone, nothing to do."

Something almost like hurt or anger flickers across his features. "You have me." He shoves the spoon back to my lips, pressing until I open up, not caring that yogurt drips down my chest.

I quickly chew and swallow before continuing with incredulity. "I have you. An orderly. Someone who comes to check on me once in a while. Someone who makes sure I eat and don't *kill* myself. I need more. I'm in here all day, all alone. I need… I don't know. Some kind of stimulation. Fresh air. Other people."

He shoves another spoonful to my lips. "I can't give you the last two—"

"Why not?" I say, leaning away from the spoon.

Ignoring my interjection, he continues, "But I can find you something to read. Would that help?"

"Why not, Dorin?" I repeat. "I need to know. What is

this place?"

His tone sharpens as I once again pull away from the prodding spoon. "Eat."

"No!" A sudden burst of frustration—maybe helplessness—makes me shove at his arm, yogurt splashing across my thighs and the padded floor.

I freeze as I realize what I've done. The last time I did this, he put me in the straitjacket and filled all my holes.

He gets up, and my lips part as I stare at him, trying to figure out what to say. Grabbing the bowl, he moves toward the door. Leaving.

"I'm sorry," I blurt, suddenly anxious about him leaving—him being mad at me. He's my only company. "Don't leave."

Fuck, I really am going insane.

Dorin doesn't spare me a glance. He just presses his finger to the biometric scanner and leaves.

I sit there, staring baffled at him for several minutes before I drop my head in defeat. Then I remain like that for several more minutes, not knowing what else to do, until the beep of the scanner makes me jolt upright.

The door opens, and Dorin steps inside. Relief, shame, defeat, and anticipation swamp me in a whir of conflicting emotions as I see what he's carrying under his arm.

The straitjacket.

"I promise I'll behave," I say, scooting back on the mattress. But even as my body throbs with the urge to get away, my skin buzzes with another need that has been simmering deep within me for days. When Dorin sets the bowl of breakfast aside and moves to sit behind me, I don't try to get away. I barely even struggle as he grabs my arm and shoves it into a sleeve. I tell myself it's because his harsh grip snuffs out my resistance, but really, it's something else.

My breaths come quicker and louder as he traps both my arms in the closed sleeves, buckles the jacket on the back, then straps my arms into place, wrapped around me in a locked position. He finishes by pushing me down to lie on the mattress and pulling the front strap between my legs. His big hand brushes my sensitive lips on the way, making sparks crackle in my nerves. But that's it. No attachments or anything. He just fastens the strap at the back, locking my pussy up, lonely and unused.

When he pulls me up to sit, I feel flustered and hot. Needy and wanting.

He drags his hand down my arm, my waist, and settles on my hips—his warm hand on my bare skin. I want him so bad I can't seem to think straight.

"Dorin, I-I—"

"What?" This time, his voice is gentle, the irritation gone.

"I—Will you please…" I trail off, unable to say I want him.

"What is it?"

I sigh, slumping in the jacket. "Nothing." I desperately want to feel him, but I can't bear the humiliation if he says no, and I can't bear the humiliation of knowing I asked for it when he crosses all the lines and breaks me apart.

He pulls me into him—his strong, wide chest and warm body. Draping an arm over my stomach, he holds me close while leaning his chin on my shoulder and lifting the spoon with a scoopful of yogurt and fruit. "Eat, little songbird."

Disappointment turns in my belly, but I open anyway and sink into him. At first, it's defeat that has me slumping, but as I sit there, enclosed in his protective embrace—under his strict control in the straitjacket—I feel oddly cared for. It's like the helplessness calms my head when combined with the irrational safety I feel in his arms.

Once the bowl is empty, he wraps his other arm around me too. Then we just sit there. Our breaths sync as we melt together, breathing each other in and soaking up the feeling of our perfectly connected bodies. I feel it; he feels it too, this bond that has grown and manifested. Everything we share. The scars, the loneliness, the intimacy of him saving me from myself, and the intensity when he took me from myself, broke me down, and freed me.

I want to put voice to it all, but for the same reasons I don't ask him to touch me, I can't. So I remain still, and the quiet comfort is all I get.

Dorin leaves me in the straitjacket, and when he returns sometime later, he has a book with him that he reads out loud to me before feeding me again. I'm not sure how long he stays, but it's much longer than usual, as if he actually listened and cared about my loneliness. Maybe an hour or so. He holds me close like he did before, caressing me and making me feel safe.

When he finally gets up to leave, he still hasn't removed the straitjacket.

"You know, I'm not gonna be any more trouble. You can take this off," I say with a small smile, glancing down at the stiff, white material.

The corners of his lips tip up in a small smile that lights up his eyes. "I kind of like you like this." His gaze trails down my restrained arms, the straps at my waist, and the one between my legs. I swear I see some kind of hunger darkening his expression just before he turns and leaves.

He wants me.

* * *

I feel a bit like a smitten teenager as I sit in my cell after Dorin's gone, and I find myself choosing pretty love songs as I sing. The feeling of going insane has faded somewhat, even despite being confined to a straitjacket like a mad person. It didn't feel like Dorin put the straitjacket on me to subdue a crazy person. It felt… possessive.

The thought makes me rock along to the rhythm of the song as hope grows inside me. It's a dangerous hope, but one I can't help but clinging to. Because unlike Zoltan, Dorin's obsession is not just about my voice or my pretty face. It reaches much deeper.

A slow scraping makes me look toward the door. The hatch, which the orderlies never use, is open, and a pair of curious eyes are looking at me through it. The person doesn't do anything, just watches.

“Who are you?” I ask in Russian. The guards here speak all kinds of languages, some Russian too, so I usually start in my mother tongue. When I don’t get a response, I shift to English. “Who are you?” Still no answer, so I add, “A new orderly?”

I have a hunch that’s not the case. The eyes look soft and feminine. Innocent, unlike all the hardened men who usually come in here.

The woman on the other side of the door confirms my hunch with a shake of her head.

“A doctor?” I ask, hope sparking within me. “Or a therapist? Is he finally letting me get some real treatment?”

A frown draws a furrow between the thin brows. She’s clearly neither a doctor nor a therapist. I guess that was only hopeful thinking from the beginning. Her behavior would be quite strange for someone working here. There’s only one possibility that makes sense. I get up and approach her, smiling softly, as I ask, “Or are you a patient too?”

She steps back as I reach the door. Leaning against it, I peer out through the opening. What I see almost makes me gasp. The person out there is a woman indeed, and she’s naked like I usually am. Except for one single item. A wide piece of leather covers her whole jaw in a snug fit. Straps go over each side of her nose, connecting into a single one that goes over her head, and two more keep the mask in place at the sides. I can’t even begin to imagine why she’s wearing it. To keep her quiet? Or keep her from biting? Then why is she roaming free like this? Has she somehow snuck off?

A foreboding sense tightens my stomach, but I ignore it, knowing it's not this girl I need to be afraid of. She looks harmless. Timid and nervous if anything. As I keep watching the mask, embarrassment seems to tighten her expression, making her eyes flicker back and forth.

"No need for embarrassment," I say, giving a small chuckle to try and lighten the mood. But I find that shame rears its ugly head inside me as I add, "I'm in a straitjacket." I've been in this thing all day, and some of the orderlies have even helped me to the bathroom without me thinking much about it. Then again, they're always cold and indifferent. Somehow, having this girl seeing it makes me see it from the outside in a way I haven't for a long time—a straitjacket, a padded cell, locked up at this facility because I'm in danger to myself.

We stare at each other for a moment, and something unspoken seems to pass between us. A shared understanding.

It makes me want to open up. I badly crave a connection to someone other than Dorin, and seeing her embarrassment at her predicament makes me bare my innermost vulnerabilities. Averting my gaze, I say, "I'm on suicide watch." I glance back at her. "At least, so I think. They don't really tell me much." I change direction, hoping she might offer me some of the answers Dorin refuses to give. "Have you been in a padded cell too? Do you get to roam free when you get out?"

She shakes her head once, then repeats. *No and no.*

"Do you get electrotherapy too? And straitjackets?" I

ask, my voice falling as I feel the defeat of it all. Shame burns inside me as I add the next question, but I hope this girl will somehow alleviate the humiliation. "And do they touch you inappropriately too?"

She lifts a finger and shakes her head. I'm not quite sure what she means until she lifts another finger and shakes her head again. *She's answering my questions.* Holding up a third finger, she gives me the answer I need the most. A long affirmative nod confirms that they use her sexually too.

Fear drops into my stomach, and there's that foreboding sense again. I want to ask the question that has been swirling in my mind since the night I had that horrible dream: *Is this actually a mental facility?* But once again, I ignore it, not daring to face the consequence of a shake of her head. So instead of fishing for more information, I search for common ground.

"Do you like it? I mean... the way they touch you? Do you come?" I bite my lips together as I realize how I'm once again confessing how *broken* I am. Even so, I keep going. "It feels wrong, doesn't it? The methods they use here? But somehow, it seems to work."

I drop my eyes to the padded floor, hating how badly I'm missing Dorin's touch and the shameful things he's made me endure. My heart suddenly aches horribly with the need, and at that moment, I'm not sure if it truly is Dorin I want or if it's because it's the only kind of connection I'm getting in this barren, empty place. Tears well in my eyes, and I don't even try to hold them in as fingers come through the hatch and brush my cheek.

Looking up, I find the girl having moved close. Her

eyes are soft and sympathetic as she gives a slow nod. Her brows lift slightly. It's almost as if she's saying that she gets it. That it's okay.

A weight lifts from my chest, and everything feels a bit lighter. I'm about to thank her when she suddenly looks off to the side, seeming to remember something. She's clearly not supposed to be here, and now she's leaving.

"Will you be back?" I ask.

She looks me over and nods. It's an uncertain confirmation, but it's there—she wants to, but she's not sure she can.

"Do it after lunch if you can," I say. "The orderlies rarely come in here at that time. I think they're on a break of their own. I don't want you to get in trouble."

She nods again, this time more eagerly. Then her hands move up to close the hatch. Just as she begins to pull it shut, I add, "My name is Lavinia, by the way. I wish I could know yours."

She considers for a moment, a wealth of uncertainty and heavy emotion passing over her face as her head seems to be working overtime. Then she looks down at her arm, and the uncertainty draws back somewhat. I breathe as quietly as possible as she hovers, seeming to debate something with herself.

Her nostrils flutter with a heavy sigh as she lifts her right arm and holds the underside up. I gasp at the sight of a small but prominent tattoo that stands out on her pale skin. *DAX001* it says. The mark speaks more than words, tightening the quiet bond that has already grown between us. Someone marked her just like they marked me. I wonder if she's here for the same reason as me—if she tried to take her own life too. Or maybe she went mad from the abuse. Maybe she'd scream or speak in tongues if they removed the mask.

Something about the idea doesn't seem right, though. She doesn't look crazy. If anything, she looks... I stare at her face as she watches the mark, and I realize she looks peaceful.

Maybe this place isn't so bad after all. Their methods are warped and illicit, but they seem to work. This woman in front of me seems to have found peace with the trauma that is haunting her, and I seem to be doing the same—to some extent.

"I have marks too," I say, looking down at the ugly scars on my thighs. When she leans close to the hatch, I lift a leg to let her see. The light in here is dim, but the horrific pattern is too vivid for her not to see. The way her breaths grow heavier reveals all too clearly that she's seeing the shame and worthlessness written across my skin quite clearly.

"A man I was with..." I trail off, closing my eyes and breathing hard before continuing. "He promised me everything, but this was what I got. He used to cut me with a knife, just for the fun of it. Stubbed out his cigars on my skin. I'm sorry someone hurt you too."

Looking up, I meet her gaze again, but instead of finding the shared understanding I expect, her expression is tight. She seems almost angry as she backs away from the door. Pointing at the tattoo on her arm, she shakes her head, and her brows lower as her anger seems to intensify. And then she runs away.

"No, don't go. I'm sorry," I call out through the hatch. I have no idea what I said to cause her reaction, but whatever it is, I'm sorry for it. "Please, come back," I say again, rising on tiptoes to call out through the opening, then dropping back onto my heels to spy after her and repeating in a whisper, "Please come back." I stand there for several minutes, barely breathing as I listen for the gentle taps of her feet against the stone floor, but she doesn't return.

17

LAVINIA

When Dorin comes to my cell sometime after the masked girl left, he's wearing a furious expression. "Who's been here? Did anyone bother you?"

At first, I don't understand, watching him with confusion.

He points behind him to the door. "The hatch. Who the hell was here? The guar—People know not to bother you. Did they speak to you? Hurt you? Touch you?" His voice is raw with violence at those last two words, and I reflexively scoot back on the mattress even though I'm clearly not the one he's mad at.

"No, no one touched me," I say breathily.

"Then who the hell was here?"

I don't know why the idea of someone coming here and talking to me bothers him so much. His reaction feeds the gnawing worry in my gut, but I don't get to consider it further.

"Who was it?" he demands.

Too shocked to think, I'm almost about to blurt that it was another patient, but my brain kicks into gear in time. "An orderly," I say. "H-he came to check if I needed a bathroom break, and then someone else came and talked to him, and he forgot to close the hatch."

He watches me with suspicion for a moment before the tight lines on his forehead soften. "Goddamn idiot. I told them not to use the fucking hatch."

I breathe a heavy sigh when Dorin lets the subject go. For some reason, I hate lying to him, but I'm more than grateful I did when the girl with the muzzle returns a few days later.

The first thing I do when the hatch opens and I see her is to apologize.

Wrapping a blanket around my shoulders, I push up. "I'm so sorry if I said something to offend you." I go to stand near the hatch. "I really didn't mean to. Please believe me. Please stay." Even though Dorin has been coming in here more often lately, reading and talking to me, I'm starved for company—any kind of mental stimulation, really. More so, there's something about this girl that makes me want to talk to her. A soft disposition and a vulnerability that seems to match my own.

I release a breath I didn't realize I was holding when she reaches a hand through the hatch to touch my palm, her eyes round and soft with something unspoken. An *it's okay,* I think.

I close my hand around hers. "How long have you been here?" I ask to start a conversation—or, open up for whatever communication is possible since she's still wearing the leather mask.

She seems almost as eager as I for company as she stays and listens, answering my questions as well as she can.

After a while, she even gestures to me, wanting me to sing to her, which, of course, I'm happy to do.

I sing a lullaby that my mother taught me, both to soothe her and myself. When the last note rings out, she's resting her head close to the hatch, her eyes dreamy and distant, and I feel calmer myself.

She gives a long nod as if to thank me. Then she points to my mouth and lifts her shoulders. When I don't understand, she does the same again.

"If I like singing?" I try.

She shakes her head, then makes a motion that has me leaning in to see her hand move up from one invisible point to another as if saying, child, teenager, and adult.

"How old was I when I started?" I guess.

She nods.

"I've been singing forever." A smile tugs at my lips as I remember singing with my mother and sister. "Music is in my blood. I played the violin too when I was a child, but then..." I trail off as I remember how I lost everything in the fire that took my home and the only two people who ever mattered to me. "I lost it," I say, and she must see the deep regret on my face as she reaches in to stroke my cheek.

"Thank you," I tell her, grateful for the comfort. "I love singing, but I really miss the violin sometimes. Moving my fingers across the strings, the smooth glide of the bow, and the vibrations. It really was something..." I let the dream sweep me away for a moment before I ask, "Have you ever played an instrument?"

She shakes her head, then lifts her hand, pointing at her ear with a smile glittering in her eyes.

"You like to listen?" I ask.

She nods eagerly, but then her expression grows somber—full of longing.

"There's not much music around here," I say.

She responds with a wistful sigh.

"Do you want me to sing some more?" I offer.

Her expression lights up as she nods, and I end up singing three songs to her before she has to leave.

During the next couple of weeks, she comes by every few days. I have no idea how she's able to come here, and it's more than lucky that she never gets caught. I try to ask her about her situation a few times, but I don't get much information out of her. It's difficult with her wearing the mask, and I sense there's something she doesn't want me to know.

One day, I notice she isn't wearing a paper bracelet on her wrist like me.

"Why don't you have one?" I ask, holding up my right hand with the hospital bracelet.

A frown forms between her brows, but she quickly softens her expression, almost like she remembers herself. Then she responds with a seemingly unknowing shrug, but I have a feeling there's more to it that she won't divulge, even if she could.

It makes my suspicion about this place grow, and one day, something happens to make it spike even more.

I'm singing softly to her when she suddenly panics and slams the hatch shut. I can only guess what's happening, and I know for sure a minute later when steps echo in the corridor. *Someone's coming.*

My heart lodges in my throat as I lean my ear close

to the door, convinced she'll get in trouble.

"Are you Dax's special project?" a man asks.

There's a beep that makes me jump away from the door, thinking he's coming inside. But when nothing happens, I carefully move back to press my ear to the padded surface.

"I don't get why he lets you stand out here. Untied and without a leash."

A leash. Untied. What the hell is that supposed to mean?

The heavy steps of the orderly disappear, and then there's the quick thuds of her running away.

I back up and drop onto the mattress, my head spinning as I try to connect the odd dots of this place.

Things don't add up. The lack of doctors and therapists. The warped electrotherapy. The lack of clothes. The men who never speak a word to me. The way they seem to fear Dorin—a mere orderly. The degrading mask the girl wears. And those words. *Untied. A leash.*

It's like a punch to the gut as I finally face the stark truth I've been trying to deny with weak excuses and threadbare logic.

This place is not what I thought it was. I don't know how I could believe it for so long.

My entire world flips as I suddenly see it all through a different lens. Dorin never actually told me this was a hospital or tried to convince me it was. I did it all by myself. He simply didn't deny it. He never told me he was an orderly. He just didn't correct me.

Horror coalesces in my belly, making nausea rise in

my throat as I stare into the room.

If I'm not in a mental facility, then where the hell am I?

If I'm not a patient, then what the hell am I?

A captive?

18

LAVINIA

I have no idea how long I sit here, staring at the padded walls. At some point, the stunned horror turns into rage that simmers inside me, making me clench my fists and bite down on my molars. Then I just wait—for Dorin to come, so I can let it all loose on him.

When the heavy thuds of his boots echo through the hall and the scanner beeps, I shoot up, fuming as I watch the door open.

"Where the hell am I? What is this place?" I demand before I see him.

But instead of a huge bulky man with a terrifyingly cold gaze, a short, pudgy man enters. Half his face is discolored from bruises, and his grin is lewd like a hungry hyena as he approaches me.

"You really don't know what this place is?" he says.

I shake my head, backing up a step.

He stops halfway, tilting his head as he rubs his stubbled jaw. "You mean to say that *big bad* Dorin has been sheltering you all this time? Keeping you like some little pet with no idea what's going to happen to you?"

Not knowing what to say, I don't respond.

He takes my silence as confirmation, and his smile grows even wider, revealing a crooked set of yellow teeth. "This is almost too good." He takes another step, making me back up more, hitting the wall. "Let me be the one to tell you then." He closes the distance, and when I try to scoot to the side, he grabs my neck and leans into my face. "You're here to be trained like an obedient slut. Once Dorin gets tired of coddling you, you're gonna be sold to be a *good* little slave, who knows how to deliver the *best* blow job. Who knows, maybe Dorin will even remove all your teeth to make it extra nice and soft." He lifts his brows in an enthused expression.

Disbelief and horror wash over me. I shake my head. He's lying. I know this is not a mental facility, but there's no way Dorin would do *that*.

"You don't believe me?" Using his free hand, he removes his phone from his pocket and scrolls until he finds the right thing. "This is all Dorin's work."

I squeeze my eyes shut as he shoves a horrible image of a toothless girl into my face.

"Look at it," he demands, giving me a shake by the throat.

Panting through the horror, I open my eyes and look. A girl with vacant eyes stares into the camera while thick, dirty fingers part her lips to reveal a toothless mouth.

"No," I squeal, unable to believe it, unable to stand the sight.

"No? That's not up for you to decide."

"Let me go." I jerk against his hand, but he only tightens his grip. Shooting my hands up, I grab onto his arm, but it's no use. So I try the only card on my hand that means anything. "Dorin will be here any second."

"Aww, you think Dorin's gonna come save you? That's so sweet. The big bad wolf has turned into a romantic."

"He'll kill you when he finds out you've laid your hands on me." I've felt the possessiveness in Dorin, and I know it's real. I might not have grasped the full meaning of this place yet, but I know for sure that I belong to Dorin and no one else is supposed to touch me. Slowly, things start to add up—the men who all fear Dorin, never touch me—but I don't get to linger on it.

He scoffs. "I'll make sure not to do any permanent damage." He leans in to whisper into my ear. "He'll be quite pleased to see that I've learned to hit in *just* the right places." With that, he hauls me away from the wall. I'm about to scream, but before I can get a sound out, he shoves a cloth into my mouth. I try to spit it out, but he somehow manages to keep his hand over my mouth while throwing me stomach-down to the floor and straddling me. I keep fighting, using all the energy I have, but he easily ties my hands behind my back and secures the cloth in my mouth with more rope going around my head.

Then he pulls a hood over my head. "Good luck getting saved now. No one will recognize you like this. Everyone will think you're just another bitch getting what she's got coming." He drags me out of the cell and down the hall, sending cold fear through my veins as he says, "I just landed Dorin a job he won't be able to resist. He'll be preoccupied for quite a while, and I'll be long gone once he finds you. Or should I say, the remaining scraps of you."

19

DORIN

"I have a job for you," one of the guards says, catching up with me as I walk down the hall, on my way to go upstairs and feed Rex dinner.

"I have somewhere else to be."

"You'll want this one."

"I'm sure I don't."

"It's a full tooth-pulling job."

"That's Dax's job," I say and walk on. Mikhail stirred up a shitstorm when Dax recently passed a full teeth extraction over to me. Every now and then, I'll indulge myself and let the sadist within me loose, even knowing Mikhail will have a fit, but I'm not stupid; if I do it too often, the damage I cause will outweigh my value, and I'll be out of here.

"Not this one," the guard counters. "The buyer wants to see it done. Without anesthetic."

I halt at this. "Are you for real?"

"Yes, the buyer is here and wants it done now."

A smile tugs at my lips. I did enjoy pulling out all that girl's teeth. I could use another job like that. It won't take more than an hour, and Rex won't die from getting dinner a little later than usual. Neither will my little songbird.

"Where?" I ask.

"Upstairs. In the trainer's lounge area."

I frown at this. No one ever brings girls upstairs—especially not that part of the building. "Why not the auction room?"

"The buyer doesn't like the basement. He prefers the view from that room."

I scoff. I've heard a lot of snobbery from buyers, but no one has ever complained about the fancy state of the auction room. Chandeliers, expensive carpets, and priceless paintings. You name it. Mikhail has gotten it all to satisfy those rich fuckers and drive the price on the girls up. But I don't think more about it. Many of those rich snobs have very specific requirements, and even though I haven't heard this one before, it's not that strange. So I follow the guard upstairs and through the corridors, past all the trainer's rooms—those who don't get a private wing like Dax, Mikhail, and me—and into the living room. In the middle of the room, a girl is bound to a chair, and some sleek idiot is lounging on the couch, nursing a glass of scotch while waiting for the show to begin.

A single set of pliers is already laid out on the shiny mahogany table beside the girl—all I need. I go to the girl and stand behind her, grabbing the pliers.

"All teeth?" I ask, glancing at the buyer.

"Every one of them," he confirms with a smirk that widens his mouth into a big grin but doesn't quite conceal the nervousness in his wide eyes.

"You know, I saw this thing the other day, on the dark web," he starts as I force the girl's jaw open and close the pliers around the first tooth. Her scream drowns out his words, but he's still talking as I drop the tooth in the golden bowl on the table and the screaming turns to hyperventilation. His blabbering is ruining the kick I usually get out of these things.

While waiting for the girl to calm somewhat, not wanting to ruin it even more by her passing out, I try to tune out his ridiculous bragging. Something about a woman being tortured and him having paid to have her beaten up and something about him having shot a dog. He talks like he's a big deal with big balls, having seen all kinds of shit. Glancing at him, I see that half of it is lies—at least the big-balls part of it. He winces as I once again grab a tooth with the pliers and start pulling, and his face grows paler with every minute as I pull out the next three teeth.

Something's off about this. Needing to find out what, I try to get him to say something that might give me a few clues.

"How did you find this place?" I ask.

"Through the dark web."

I cast him a sideways glance. There's no way he found this place online. This place is well hidden, and every person who knows about it also knows not to mention anything online if they want to stay alive. Even if that wasn't the case, his tapping foot gives him away. I don't have to be Mikhail to tell that shit. This guy is transparent as fuck.

"How did you really find it?"

"I told you, the dark web," he says, this time adding a nervous chuckle.

I shake my head. Even the dumbest idiot guard we have here could tell this guy is lying. Tightening my grip on the girl's head, I grip another tooth and yank hard. Deepening my voice, I hold up the pliers with her tooth as I watch him. "How did you find this place?"

His face turns pale as a ghost as he stares from the tooth to my face, eyes blinking repeatedly. "Are you deaf?" he finally says, trying to act all tough.

With a sigh, I drop the tooth into the bowl and cross the room. The guy tries and fails to remain fully upright as I approach him. Grabbing his jaw, I apply enough pressure that his mouth pops open. Before he knows what's hit him, I have the pliers deep in his mouth, grabbing one of his molars.

"How. Did. You. Find. This. Place."

"Aaa iin," he squeals, squirming on the couch and flailing his hands. The tumbler drops to the floor and shatters around my boots as I give a little pull. He squeals like a pig, almost as loud as the girl. *What a pussy.* I barely jostled the tooth.

Removing the pliers, I try one final time. "Where?"

"My friend," he gushes. "He-he told me he knew this place wh-where they do all kinds of crazy shit to women. He had gotten this deal. Some guy named Jan. He couldn't come here himself so soon, so he offered me the deal. If he would..."

I don't stay to hear what kind of deal his friend made. I'm bolting the moment I hear Jan's name fall over his lips. *That little shithead; I should have killed him.* I run as fast as I can, through the castle, down the basement stairs, and through the halls, until I reach cell one. It seems to take forever for the scanner to register my finger, and I'm sweating and panting as I shove the door open and barge into her cell, ready to kill. But no one's there. It's empty.

For a second, I just stand there, flitting my eyes across the room as if I could find her in one of the crevices of the padded walls.

Then I'm running again. Down the hall, barking at the first guard I see. "Where's Jan?"

"No idea."

"Fucking find him."

I rip the door open to the first whipping room in the next corridor. Empty. I try the next door to find a guy fucking a tied-up girl.

"Find Jan," I demand and rush on. I open every door in the corridor and bark orders at two more guards before I reach the next hall. Then I open all the cell doors there, but all I find are cowering or screaming girls. My songbird and Jan are nowhere to be found. I'm halfway through the cells in the third corridor when I remember the unused rooms in the derelict halls.

My boots pound against the ground as I run there, my heart beating even harder. My vision blurs with a potent mix of rage and terror as I rip the first door open with a force that has the old door falling half off its hinges. I nearly slam my fist into it when I find the cell empty, but a scream stops me. I halt and listen, not wanting to waste a second more on empty rooms.

There it is again, pained and *hers*. I can recognize

her voice anytime, anywhere. It's coming from across the hall. A few cells down. I bolt in that direction and rip a new door open. And there, in the old, dingy room, I see the worst thing I've witnessed in all of my brutal life.

My sweet songbird, bruised and bound, face drawn tight in agony. Angry red stripes cover her thighs, her breasts, and what little of her ass I can see. Blue bruises are already forming around them, and blood trickles down her milky white skin in several places.

But the marks don't even compare to the horror of the situation I've walked in on. The caning is already over, the instrument discarded on the floor. And Jan is deep inside her ass, fucking her. Taking what belongs to *me.*

Time slows to an agonizing slow motion as the fucker turns his head and says with a wide grin, "She's so deliciously tight. It's a shame you didn't get to break in the whore yourself."

Tunnel vision narrows my focus, anger reddening my sight.

I cross the room, grab his neck, and snap it.

It happens so quickly the shock barely registers on his face before he's dead.

His cock falls out of her as he drops to the ground.

She has gone silent, swaying in the ropes, eyes staring straight ahead as if she were dead. For a moment, I almost think she is.

"Lavinia," I demand, grabbing her face. "Look at me. It's me, Dorin. You're safe now."

She blinks but doesn't focus on me.

It's reassurance enough. I need to get her down, then

I can get her back to me.

I grab the switchblade in my pocket and slice through the ropes keeping her restrained to the ceiling hook, cursing at the sight of blood lacing the rough material that is wound way too tight around her wrists. With a hand around her waist, I catch her weight as she collapses, limp and boneless, devoid of hope.

Carefully, I lower her to the floor and cut the ropes from her wrists and legs. Then I hurriedly move to sit beside her and stroke the blonde tresses from her sweat-streaked face.

"Please do that to..." Her words fade into a murmur I can't discern.

Leaning down, I place my ear close to her mouth. "Say that again."

She clears her throat and says in a raspy voice, "Will you please do that to me too?"

Leaning back, I watch her with a frown. "What, my pretty songbird? What do you need me to do?"

"Snap my neck," she says with more power, coughing as the effort strains her tired throat.

I almost ask her to repeat the words, not wanting to believe what I just heard. But the words were loud and clear. There's no doubt she said what I think she did. I shouldn't be surprised after the way I initially found her, but still, everything inside me crumbles. I glance behind her, at the dead man sprawled on the floor, his limp dick sticking out of his pants. Anger swells, and I wish I could breathe life into him so I could kill him again—in a much more painful way.

"No," I say in a firm voice.

She reaches out for me, her small hand trembling as she tries to grab onto my jeans. "Please, Dorin, I—"

"No," I cut her off and push up, away from her. The anger keeps coiling, twisting, and turning, expanding and breathing fury into my muscles. I want to snap her neck just for asking that. I'm afraid I'll actually do it if I stay and she repeats those words. So I leave. I walk out of the room, slam the door, and pace halfway down the derelict corridor as if the door isn't enough to block the sound of her frail voice.

Rubbing my hand against my scalp, I stare down the empty hall, listening to the empty silence.

People always say the silence comes before the storm, but no one talks about the silence that comes after the storm. The gut-wrenching grief and the lonely anger that threatens to dredge up new whirlwinds and crackling thunder. It keeps building, simmering, and churning, quiet and deadly.

I clench and unclench my hand at my side until something within me snaps. Spinning on my heel, I raise my fist and slam it into the nearest door. My blood buzzes with the need to go find a motherfucker to take my rage out on. Maybe the arrogant prick upstairs. Or Mikhail for not letting me kill Jan in the first place.

I stare from the gaping hole in the thick wooden door to my bleeding knuckles, then down the hall from where I came. Suddenly, I don't want to hit something or someone. I want to hold. *Her.*

As I trudge back, the livid energy dissipates. In its stead comes a heavy defeat that settles upon my back like a hundred-ton boulder. Suddenly, I feel tired to the bone.

I just want to lie down and take my little songbird in my arms, kiss away her pain, and rock us both to sleep.

But as I enter the room, a new burst of adrenaline shoots through me.

My quiet songbird, who was deadly still when I left her, is now banging the back of her head against the unforgiving stone floor.

"Stop!" I bark, rushing to her and shoving my hand under her head to block the impact. The force of her movement is startling. If my knuckles weren't already bloody, they would be now.

Lifting her head again, she angles it away from my hand and slams it down again, aiming for the hard ground.

"No, no, no, what are you doing?" I say with horror as I move my hand in to soften the blow. With my other hand on her forehead, I block her head from moving as she tries to lift it again.

Tears gather in her unfocused eyes. "Just let me die," she says in a broken voice so full of sorrow and defeat that it burns my heart.

"No," I say with a force that gives rise to a surge of anger in her.

Throwing her hands up, she shoves at my arm and starts writhing. When she can't get her head free, she starts clawing at her own skin, drawing new bloody trails across her stomach.

"Stop it," I demand, moving my hand out from under her head to grab her hands. As I restrain her arms, she starts kicking and scraping her feet against the rough ground instead. "Stop!" I demand as I climb on top of her, but she keeps going, hurting herself as much as she possibly can.

This girl truly wants to die. The merciful thing to do would be to snap her neck. But I don't do merciful. I'm selfish and ruthless. So I flip her onto her stomach, crawl on top of her, and trap her arms under her as I lower my weight onto her. With my feet pressed to her legs, I stop her kicking, and with an arm banded around her chest and a hand under her forehead, I block her head from moving.

She gives a few more jerks, but I have her fully immobilized, and soon, her fight drains, and grief overcomes her. Hollow sobs rack through her, making her shake beneath me, and tears trickle down her cheeks, dripping onto the stony floor.

"I've got you," I reassure, kissing the wet trails and rocking her as much as I can in the awkward position. "Jan can't harm you anymore. He's dead."

My words only seem to spur her grief. Her sobs grow more anguished, her breathing more labored.

"Just kill me," she repeats in a voice devoid of hope. "Please"—she shudders as she tries to inhale—"kill me."

"No." I glance to the side to see a bundle of ropes on the floor. It's only a few feet away. If I can just get her arms and legs tied, I can get her back to her cell safely. But as I try to reach for it, she somehow wrests her arm free and starts clawing at her skin again. If only she would scratch at me instead, I wouldn't care, but seeing her hurt herself like this has me perplexed, furious, and feeling helpless in a way I never have before.

"Stop!" I yell and grab her tightly again, realizing I'm

not going anywhere anytime soon. But I need to get her back to her cell—under thick blankets on a soft surface. Her skin is cold, and the floor must be scraping her skin each time she jerks against me. So when I hear footfalls in the distance, I roar for whoever it is to come down here.

"Get me a tranquilizer. Now!" I add as a guard appears at the door.

The guard rushes off, and within two minutes, he returns, handing me a syringe. Wasting no time, I bite the plastic cap off and jab the syringe into her neck. The few seconds it takes for the sedative to kick in are too long. Any amount of time seeing my songbird in such agony is too long.

"That's it," I croon into her ear as she goes slack beneath me.

"Please kill me," she whispers one more time before the drug drags her down.

Carefully, I lift her to sit, supporting her listless body against me as I check the back of her head. An angry wound has me clenching my teeth. I'll need to make a stop at Dax's office to have him check on her before taking her back to her cell.

"Clean this up," I order, gesturing toward Jan's dead body. The guard is still standing in the doorway, scurrying to the side like a scared squirrel as I lift my songbird into my arms and head for the door. I pause three steps down the hall and turn. "On second thought, drag him into the main hall and let him lie there for a couple of days as a reminder of what will happen to anyone who touches my girl."

20

LAVINIA

Something is pounding. A constant war drum going off in my head, expanding and growing louder as I slowly come to.

I try to keep my eyes closed and drift back to sleep, but new pains flare in my body as the thick fog lifts. My whole backside is burning, bruises and scrapes all over my body are stinging, and my wrists are screaming from the raw sores circling them.

The worst pain is not the one on the outside, though, or even the searing sensation throbbing in my back opening. No, what has me wailing into the room is the flare of memories. Painful, brutal, heart-shattering memories and realizations.

The helplessness of being bound and beaten, the worthlessness of being reduced to a whore, and the soul-shattering sensation of a man forcing his erection into my ass, clawing along my dry walls, and invading me in the most dehumanizing way possible. But not even that is the worst thing. It's just another straw on the already broken camel's back. What has me releasing another clawing scream is the betrayal. The crushed hope.

How cruel can this world be? After everything I've lost and endured, I finally worked up the nerve to forge my escape and slit my wrists. And just when I was about to leave, I was swept away. Into another hell, where the flames burn twice as hot and the devil's claws scrape twice as deep.

Out there, I got raped and abused, but I was always free to roam on and escape one hell; in here, I'm trapped in ways I could have never imagined. Trapped within narrow halls where beasts roam. Nowhere to run, nowhere to hide. Trapped in this padded cell, forced to endure this stagnant life. No choice, no chance. Just trapped.

I can't accept it. I just can't. I won't.

I stare down at my wrists and the scars the knife left—the one I wielded. Why couldn't I do it? Why am I so weak?

A new wave of anger wells inside me, this time directed at myself. It crashes with all the fury at the world and every cruel thing it has to offer. I can't accept that I'm stuck here. I can't accept my weakness. I need to end this. Somehow, any way I can.

I gnash my teeth together as I watch the blue veins beneath my skin. I might not have a knife, but I have something else. If only I am strong enough, I can end things right here and now. I can escape.

With a sharp inhale, I gather all my will and sink my teeth into my wrist.

21

DORIN

I wake in the middle of the night, cold sweat beading on my brow and heart pounding in my chest. I haven't woken from a nightmare since I beat my father to death when I was fifteen and retook the power he had stolen from me.

I can't even remember what I dreamed, but an acute sense of unease crawls across my skin even as I turn the lights on, leave the bed, and get dressed.

Rex gives a slow whine as he gets up from the rug beside the bed and follows me through the living room to the kitchen area. I grab a few pieces of cold cuts from the fridge, throw him one, and stuff the rest into my mouth.

"You'll get fat and lazy if I feed you every time you look at me like that," I tell him as he keeps staring at me expectantly. Leaning down to scratch him behind the ear, I add, "Go back to bed. I have something I need to check on."

His paws scrape against the floor as he follows me to the door. I've trained him well enough that he knows not to go farther without permission, so he settles for giving me another wide-eyed stare as I step into the hall.

I have no idea how the big dog with a bark that can scare even the worst of men got so cuddly. It's not just food he shamelessly begs for.

"Not now, buddy." I sigh and close the door.

As I make my way to the basement, an image pops into my head: Rex lying beside the fragile woman in the padded cell, cuddling up against her as she lies there in the straitjacket, sad and broken, and her burrowing her face into his soft fur as she weeps. I'm sure he would love to provide comfort like that, and I think she just might love it too.

My mind wanders. I imagine lying down behind her, taking turns stroking his fur and her golden locks, listening to their breathing slowing down as they both fall asleep. I would drift away quickly too.

A sense of dread pulls me from the peaceful images as I open the heavy door leading into the dungeon. An urgent feeling that something is wrong keeps tugging at me, getting worse with each step I take toward the hall with the padded cells. It keeps gnawing and twisting to the point where I run.

My gut feeling is always right. It's like some kind of bad déjà vu as I rip the door to her cell open. There, in the middle of the floor, sits the blue-eyed woman with the milky white skin and blonde hair. Instead of the white tiles of the night I found her, the walls are covered in white padding. But even this room can't protect her from herself. Just like that first night, there's blood. It's not as violent or pervasive, filling the tub and staining the walls, but the trail of red down her arm is just as frightening as she digs her teeth into her wrist.

Shocked, I hover. It's only for a moment, but that second seems to stretch out into an agonizingly slow minute as dread pulses in my heart. Snapping out of it, I burst through the room, digging my fingers into her jaw and shoving her to the floor.

"Get off me," she wails as I pin her, stomach-down, grabbing her arm to inspect the damage. The bite wound is deep. So deep that blood would've been pulsing from her veins if she had bitten a little more to the left. I'm almost impressed she had the strength to do this. Most people couldn't hurt themselves even if their lives depended on it—even less to take their own life. But the awe drowns in horror as I realize how close I came to walking in on her bleeding out. If I had come just a minute later, she might have bit again and hit the right vein.

"I've got you," I say absently as I tighten my grip on her hands to keep her still. It's all I can do to try and calm her as guilt rattles through my mind and the only thought I can think is, *Why the fuck didn't I put her in the straitjacket.*

"I hate you. I fucking hate you!" she screams as she struggles. "Just kill me!"

"No," is all I can say as I try to chase away the horror of how close she came to taking her own life. On my watch.

I don't get much time to process. As she starts banging her head against the floor, I'm forced to act. I don't even get time enough to remember that she can't hurt herself on the padded floor before I've pulled a syringe from my pocket and stabbed it into her neck. My brain only kicks in when she goes slack beneath me and murmurs in a broken voice, full of bone-deep hurt, "I trusted you."

I pause, the syringe butt halfway down. Part of me wants to inject the rest and go back upstairs and sleep, but those words do something to me. For some reason, I can't stand to leave like this—her hating me. That last part wins out. I withdraw the needle and lift her onto the mattress, arranging her slack limbs carefully as I place her on her back.

"I've got you," I say again, this time more sincerely, as I stroke the hair from her face. "I'll fix you. Just like I did when I found you."

Her blue eyes fill with disbelief and grief as she blinks up at me, struggling to keep them open.

"I—" She opens her mouth to speak again, but her words are slow and staggered. "I fucking..."

I spit on two fingers and position them at her opening. I had decided not to touch her, not wanting to ruin her, but someone else did that, so what does it matter now? If that wasn't enough, her pleas for me to take her life infuriate me more than I understand, making me want to punish her.

"I fucking hate y—"

Slamming my fingers inside her, I cut off her pathetic attempt at throwing vehemence at me. "You hate me? Is that it?"

She makes a weak nod, her eyes going round at the sudden intrusion.

"Are you sure?" I pump my fingers in and out at a fast pace, making her twitch on the mattress. She feebly tries to push at my arms, but I simply slap her hands away.

Nodding, she lets out a whimper that sounds like more pain than pleasure. I'll remedy that in a second, but first, I want her to suffer for hating me so damn much—or thinking that she does.

Leaning over her, I grab her throat and squeeze until her breaths come in wheezes. "If I leave, I can't kill you," I say, tilting my head as I stare at her.

"P-please," she manages.

"Please what?" I mock. "Leave or kill you?" I press my thumb to her clit, relishing the tiny mewl of pleasure coming out of her throat.

Her eyes flicker between mine, uncertainty filling the dazed blue of her gaze along with pleasure.

Her mewls grow longer and more frequent as I keep pumping and dragging my thumb over her clit. Her juices coat my fingers, creating a slick sound, and her cheeks turn a pretty shade of pink. She gets so easily turned on for me. I love the sight and the sound of it.

Leaning in, I drag the tip of my tongue across the side of her mouth, a featherlight touch that sends an unmistakable moan up her throat. I repeat at the other side of her mouth, and her body starts to convulse as she nears the edge. I pull my head back to watch her lips part and her gaze go cloudy from more than the drugs.

Her eyelids flutter, and her hips press up, seeking more of my touch. A long moan that comes from deep within her gut tells me she's just about to fall over, and that's when I pull out.

"No," she gasps, staring at me with shock written

deep in those dazed eyes.

"Do you still want me to leave?" I flex my hand around her throat. "Or kill you?" I blow an exhale on the corner of her mouth, smiling to myself at the shudder that rolls through her. "It would be so easy. I could just snap your neck." I squeeze a little harder, and her feeble hands once again come up to mine, trying to push it away. "Or choke you. There's nothing you can do about it, flapping your weak hands like that."

Her staggered inhale sends a cool breeze across my lips as I slacken my grip a bit. The caress of her breath compels me to lean in and connect our mouths. Just barely. I press the slightest kiss to her lips as I stare into her terrified, turned-on eyes. I lift my hand, which is glistening from her moisture, and snap her nose closed.

"Or I could simply steal your life with a kiss. Seems poetic, doesn't it?" I've never cared for poetry or the finer things in life, but this girl makes me want to lose some of my calloused crudeness and seek out something more. So I lean down and seal her lips with mine as I invade her mouth with my tongue.

I'm not sure if this qualifies as a kiss. I wouldn't know. I've never kissed a girl—never wanted to. But my tongue roams over hers, exploring her intimate space, taking and tasting her sweet delicacy. Her helplessness.

She gives a tiny jerk, a minuscule struggle, but her tongue starts moving, nonetheless. *With* mine. She wants this even though part of her doesn't—both the kiss and the death it could bring. I indulge the latter idea for a moment, relishing her staggered attempts at breaking the connection when her air grows scarce. She jerks against me, trying to turn her head, clawing weakly at my hands and my face, but it doesn't change a thing. I have her right where I want her, and there's nothing she can do to stop me.

My cock grows achingly hard in my pants. I want to free it and come inside her while I snuff her out—or at least while she thinks I do. But there's no time. And I want to see her come even more. So I release her throat and move my hand between her legs. My grip on her nose and my tongue in her mouth are more than enough to keep her weak head in place, the seal blocking her airways tight. I slam my fingers into her again, and her walls clasp onto them like they could grant her the air she desperately needs.

Her jerking grows more desperate, and she manages to put more strength into her clawing hands as her survival instinct kicks in. Her chest shakes as she tries to breathe in fresh air, but all she gets is what little residual oxygen I'm breathing into her. Her survival instinct isn't the only thing making her jerk, though. I feel the orgasm building in her like a brewing storm. Her hips jerk, and little moans stutter in her throat, desperate for air to give them life.

Her strength weakens again as the lack of air drains the energy from her system. Her struggling hands hold on to mine instead of fighting, and her movements turn to tiny spasms. In ten seconds, she'll lose consciousness; in thirty seconds, she'll die.

A rush of power unlike any shoots through me, and I damn near come in my pants. I want to prolong this moment and bask in it forever. But five more seconds tick by, and I don't want to lose her. I want something else. Just as I break the seal and let her drag in new air, I get it.

The sweetest moan I've ever heard forms in her open mouth as her entire body tightens, making her buck up over the mattress. It's not a loud or long moan; the sound is full of sweet innocence and helplessness, freer than any sound I've ever heard. There's no force or control, trying to push or pull. It's just an instinctive, bodily reaction—like when the girls scream beneath my baton. Only this is so much better.

The orgasm rolls through her like a tiny storm, and then she's out.

I remain on top of her, staring at her, mesmerized, as she breathes soft slow breaths through slightly parted lips. It's tempting to stay here for the rest of the night, but I need more sleep, and I'm not sure she'll stay like this for long—I only gave her half of the syringe.

I inject the rest of the sedative into her neck to make sure she won't wake for the next part. Then I disinfect and bandage the self-inflicted wound on her wrist, cursing myself as I go. Finally, I carefully slip the straitjacket on her. I'm not risking anything with this girl again.

* * *

"What the hell did you do?" Mikhail barks as he approaches me in the corridor the next morning.

"Fuck you," I say and walk past him, but Mikhail, the reckless fucker, grabs my arm, making me halt.

I turn to him and stare him down. The effect is usually stuttered *yes sirs* or blabbered apologies, but Mikhail is unaffected, holding his stance, hands on his hips, eyes glaring straight back at me.

"I told you I couldn't spare to lose a trainer," he says in that annoying, berating tone, like he's my father or some shit.

"I did you a fucking favor. The guy was a goddamn liability."

"I don't give a fuck. I told you to keep him alive."

I point my finger at his face. "He fucking touched what's mine, so he dies. Let that be a fucking lesson to everyone else here."

He cocks an eyebrow. "Yours. What's the deal with this girl, anyway?"

"None of your damn business."

"The hell it isn't. You work for me. At least that's what you're supposed to do. Not spending all your time on one fucking girl, who shouldn't even be here. She's been in that padded cell for God knows how long—weeks? Months?"

Having had enough of this shit, I turn my back to him to leave.

"It's time you get rid of her. Today. Take her to the incinerator and get on with your real job. You've had enough playtime."

Ignoring him, I gnash my teeth together as I think about how Lavinia would love that.

When I keep walking, he adds, "If you don't do it, I'll have someone else take care of it."

At that, I whip around and stalk back, getting into

his face. "If something happens to her, you'll pay. I'll take you to the incinerator myself and burn you goddamn alive. Do you understand?"

Mikhail doesn't even flinch even as I lean in over him. He just looks me dead in the eye, his expression calm and collected. Then, out of nowhere, he goddamn grins. A full, wide smirk spreads over his face. "Ah, I see what's going on here. You're turning soft. Like Dax."

I scoff. Dax and I are *nothing* alike. He might be the only person I tolerate around here, but I'm nothing like him and his American arrogance.

"Here's the deal. You'll run the auction tomorrow night and cater to every little need of my customers while I go find a replacement for Jan. If they're satisfied, I'll let you keep your little pet."

"You know I don't do that shit." I fucking hate those rich assholes, and what's even worse is being at their beck and call, trying to please their ridiculous requests to drive home a good deal. I don't care about the money. Never have. Not like Mikhail and Dax, who get a fucking hard-on whenever they see a little money rolling in, despite having more than they'll ever be able to spend. It's fucking weak, is what it is.

He shrugs. "That's the deal. Take it or leave it. Or take the girl and leave."

I roll my eyes. He knows I'm never going to leave this place of my own free will. I hate that Mikhail holds that power over me, but this is the only place I've ever fit in—the only place that keeps me from going crazy. And Mikhail is the only person I respect enough to refrain from beating to a pulp when he bosses me around like this. And maybe more, I refrain because I need him here. Without him to take care of the business side of things, some other shithead would step in, or I'd have to do it myself, and that last part sure isn't going to happen. That incident with the tough-ass rich guy wanting to see a full-teeth extraction was more than enough buyer contact to last me a whole month.

And now, I have to agree to even more buyer contact. I fucking seethe, but mutter my agreement anyway. "Fine, I'll do it."

I turn to walk away, and Mikhail calls out with a smug tone, "Enjoy your pet."

"I fucking will," I mutter under my breath. *Once I find a way to rid her of her suicidal wishes and stop her from hating me.*

22

LAVINIA

The straitjacket becomes an intimate, unwanted friend during the next few days. So do the drugs. Dorin keeps me in a lethargic daze all day, all night, strapped in the straitjacket and drugged up, unable to move, unable to think, and barely able to speak.

"I hate you," I tell him in a slurred voice every time he comes into my cell.

"Shh," he simply soothes, stroking my hair out of my face or pulling me up to sit against him so he can feed me. When I beg him not to drug me again or tell him that my arms are hurting from being trapped in the same position for so long, he simply strokes me again and says, "It's for your own good. I don't want you to hurt yourself."

There's no possible way I can. I feel so weak I can barely turn on the mattress most of the time. The drugs rarely get to wear off enough to give me a clear head before he comes and shoots me up with more sedative.

One day when my head does clear enough to remember all the horrors I learned before he plunged my world into a meaningless haze, I ask him about this place of terrors and torment. "Where am I? Tell me the truth."

He remains silent as he opens the straitjacket and helps me out of it, hoists me into his arms, and brings me out of the cell. "An old castle that's been renovated to fit another purpose. Or maybe to once again fit its original one. No one really knows what this dungeon was used for."

"Selling women? Is that what you do down here?"

"We train and sell them, yes." He carries me across the hall, and the scanner on the door beeps as it registers his finger.

"How can you even—" I shut my eyes and gulp to swallow the bitterness lodged in my throat. "How can you do such a thing?"

He shrugs. "There's not much else I know how to do."

"But—" I trail my gaze over his long scar and empty expression. There's no use in asking how he can do the despicable things he does and still live with himself. The real question is, why hasn't he sold me yet? Or why hasn't he done more to train me? Those last two questions only become more confounding as he lowers me into a tub full of hot water and I look around to see that we're in a cozy bathroom—shelves on the walls, plants on the counter, and a beautiful chandelier bathing the room in a soft light.

"Why?" I choke out, blinking to hold back the tears forming in my eyes.

Crouching beside me, Dorin brushes the tears from the sides of my eyes. "Let them out."

I close my eyes hard and ask the question that's

most pressing—the one I've been postponing asking, too afraid to know the answer. The one that threatens to break the dam that I refuse to show him again. "Are you gonna sell me?"

"Yes," he says without hesitation.

"When?"

"I don't know."

"To who?"

"I don't know."

Everything inside me coils tight, squeezing my chest and making breathing hurt—making living hurt.

"Please kill me," I say, facing him again even though the tears are now pooling in my eyes. "Please, just do it. Or let me do it myself. Just leave your knife here and leave the room. I promise I'll go through with it this time. I won't even make a mess. I'll hold my wrist underwater. All the blood will remain in the tub."

Shaking his head, he grabs a sponge and starts washing me.

"Stop. Don't touch me." I push at his hand, but I'm still weak, barely managing to put any strength into the movement.

"Just let me take care of you," he says, continuing the slow motions over my stomach.

"No!" I plunge down, under the water, and grab the edges of the tub for leverage. If he won't end it or let me do it myself, the water can take me. But once again, I'm too weak. I don't even get to decide whether I take or continue my own life anymore. He simply grabs me under the arms and pulls me back up.

I flail weakly as he holds me there, one arm banded

around my chest as he removes his boots and jeans. The moment he releases me to pull off his T-shirt, I slip under again, but the few seconds it takes him to discard it isn't even enough to make me feel out of air.

Next thing I know, he's in the tub with me, stark naked, pulling me into him and trapping me against his body with one massive arm that keeps my arms locked at my sides. I kick in the water, but he simply wraps his legs over mine, and when I start banging my head into his shoulder, he presses his free hand to my forehead.

And that's it. I'm trapped. Yet I keep struggling, using up what little energy I have left. Once I've worn myself out and go limp against him, panting hard, he releases my forehead and grabs the sponge again.

"Please," I beg in a weak voice.

"Shh, just let me take care of you."

It's all so very hopeless, and I can't stop the tears from trickling down my cheeks. I manage not to make any sounds, but I'm sure he can tell from my shaking chest that I'm crying. I know for sure when he leans in to press tiny kisses to my cheek, absorbing the tears as he goes. The intimacy makes the tears flow faster, dripping into the water.

"That's it. Give them all to me. Cry for me, my little songbird," he whispers, reminding me of how Zoltan wanted my tears. The memory gives me the strength to shut them down. I curl in on myself, closing off everything. It takes all I have, leaving me cold, alone, and broken. All I want to do is give in to that gentle touch and those tender kisses—release all the heavy burdens and let him carry them for me. But I can't. Dorin is just another monster who wants to take everything I have and destroy me. I refuse to give it to him.

* * *

The days blur together, and my moments of clarity are far apart. I have no idea how long time passes in this stagnant haze. All I know is Dorin coming and going, feeding me, bathing me, drugging me, and restraining me. He's comforting and caressing me too—I think he might even be touching me sexually and making me come, but I'm never sure whether it's a dream or reality. I always shut him out when my head is clear enough to think, and no matter the amount of drugs he gives me, I never break down in front of him.

As I lie in my cell, slowly coming out of a haze, waiting for him to come and bring me into a new one, I remember that I haven't even sung for a long while. I'm not even sure I can muster the muscular strength to do so. Parting my lips, I want to try. But then again, what's the point? It doesn't matter anymore. Nothing does.

A sliding sound at the door breaks into my consciousness. *Finally, he's here to numb my brain and make me forget.*

But the door doesn't open. Instead, there's a tap. Then another one, a bit louder.

I lift my head to look, blinking to focus my blurry gaze.

The hatch is open, and there's someone on the other side, looking in. At first, I don't understand. But then recognition strikes as the head moves back a bit and I see the muzzle. *It's the girl with the tattoo.* The one who used to come here often, but hasn't been here for a while.

She lifts her hand and waves.

Slowly, I push up to sit, then put in all my strength to get to my feet and stagger to the door, all but collapsing against it.

"Did you know?" I ask, leaning my head into her hand as she reaches in to stroke my cheek. "That we're all just sex slaves? That they'll sell us?"

She nods, and her answer is like a stab in the back. But then I remember that she can't speak. She never could tell me the truth. So I shove the thought away and stare off into the distance as I soak up her comfort—the only friend I have.

"I thought he saved me." My heart breaks all over again as I remember how Dorin took me from the bloody tub, brought me here, and "cared" for me, only to have my world crash in the cruelest way possible. "I actually thought I had found someone who wanted to help me. Genuinely." A tiny laugh erupts from my mouth. *The irony of it all.* "How stupid was I? Now he keeps me drugged up and locked in this jacket, afraid I'll hurt myself." I glance into the cell—the padded walls and the lonely mattress. "How am I supposed to do that in here?"

I remember that I actually managed to do some damage, and a small sense of pride rolls through me. But it quickly drowns in the defeat of it all. There's no way to win here. It's all one slow, agonizing descent into a hell that will surely be worse than any of the previous I've known.

The quiet girl reaches her hand farther in to get

better access to my face, stroking my cheeks and temples and down the sides of my neck. It's the best thing I've felt for a long time—or maybe not quite, but all the other comfort I've had has come with a severe dish of hatred and deceit so stark I could barely breathe.

Tears form in my eyes and drip down my cheeks. For once, I don't try to stop them. But they don't escalate either. I guess I'm still too drugged up.

We stand there for a long time, wrapped in the silence, connected by the bleak despair. The world seems to stop, and I find the closest thing to peace I've felt in a while.

But then, in an instant, everything changes. She draws back with a jerk, leaving me alone and forlorn. The hatch slams shut, and the quietness becomes stifling.

Leaning my forehead against the door, I heave a shuddery breath as loneliness wraps around my lungs.

The silence only lasts a minute, and the loneliness drowns in dread as I hear heavy steps approach.

Please don't let it be Dorin, please don't let it be Dorin, is all I can think. Somehow, I just know he'll react worse than anyone else to find out she has been sneaking through the halls to see me.

Pressing a hand to my mouth, I block a gasp at the sound of Dorin's angry voice. "What the hell are you doing here?" There's a moment of silence before he adds, "You're Dax's girl." The realization only angers him more, his voice becoming furious as he says, "Is he in there?"

My heart is like a jackhammer beating through the quiet space as I wait for him to continue.

"Then why the hell are you here? Have you bothered her? Have you opened the hatch?"

The beep of the lock mechanism startles me. Before I can react, the door flies open, and I stagger as I lose the support of the padded surface. My arms strain against the straitjacket as I prepare for the fall, but Dorin catches me just before my legs give in.

A wave of dizziness clouds my vision, and I blink up at him as he holds me to him, grabbing my jaw to study my face. His expression darkens with a fury that has me shrinking. With a feral growl, he steadies me on my own two legs and turns to the girl in the muzzle. "You made her cry."

A pounding urgency thrums inside my head as I watch him approach her, unclipping a thick baton, which looks like the ones the police carry, from his belt.

"You'll pay for that," he snarls, towering over her as she retreats and crumbles to the floor as she hits the wall.

"No, Dorin, stop." Somehow, I make my legs work enough to rush forward and intercept—stepping right in front of the beast. "She comforted me," I say, staring up at him. It's only then, seeing the murderous fury in his eyes, that I realize just how reckless a move this is. Even so, I don't regret it. I couldn't live with myself, knowing I'd hurt her—the only person left that I care about.

"Get back to your cell." Dorin pushes me aside, aiming his furious gaze at the poor girl who's huddled up on the ground against the wall, shaking worse than my unsteady legs.

"She helped me," I implore. "Please, just leave her be."

Relief is a brief gust of wind as Dorin turns to me. Grabbing my arm, he steers me back toward my cell, but only to snap a hook to the back of the straitjacket and connect it to an eye in the wall, rendering me useless and helpless.

"*Don't* fucking bang your head against the wall, or I'll shoot you up with so many drugs that all you can do is drool out your fucking mouth."

I've never seen him like this. The anger in his eyes is menacing, the threat in his voice so brutal I forget about the huddling girl for a moment. Gulping, I nod my understanding. I don't think I'd dare to bang my head against the wall even if I thought it would actually kill me before he could stop me.

The world flashes before me as Dorin turns and stalks across the hall, growling, "No one hurts what's mine."

Dizziness has me shuffling to stay upright, the hook catching me as I'm about to fall forward. I fall back against the wall and watch the blurry silhouette of Dorin's figure lean down toward the scared girl. I want to scream, but I'm stuck—frozen in place, hyperventilating, and so weak I can barely give voice to any sound.

A jolt of pins and needles has me gasping as a sharp voice cuts through the hall.

"Stop!" someone demands, the sound of hard heels echoing against the walls as someone approaches.

Turning my head, I see a tall figure stop a few feet from Dorin. My vision finally clears, and I see a sleek, controlled man with sharp features and a trimmed beard, dressed in a black silk shirt and dress pants. He oozes a kind of quiet, deadly power that has me shuddering as he says with powerful authority, “Don’t touch her.”

To my surprise, Dorin pauses. “She made my girl cry.”

My eyes fly down to his hand fisted in the girl’s hair and to her frightened eyes. The vision snaps me out of the haze. “She didn’t. She didn’t make me cry.” I jerk against the straitjacket, needing to get to her—to stop Dorin, to comfort her. But the hook holds me in place, and neither man casts me a single glance.

The sleek man, who seems to be the one in charge, makes a call on his phone and fires off a few quick words. “Cell one, now. It’s your girl.” Then he’s off the phone again, pointing a warning finger at Dorin. “You’d better not put a single scratch on her. She’s Dax’s girl, and you know the deal.”

Dax. The name swirls in my brain, wanting me to remember something. I can’t figure out what before a new voice breaks into the space.

“Get the fuck off her!”

It’s the long-haired man, who came into the medical room the first time Dorin gave me electrotherapy. His eyes are as murderous as Dorin’s, and a new type of urgency has me pulling to get free as he goes straight for Dorin, fist raised into the air.

Just before he can strike, Dorin releases the cowering girl and steps aside.

The man, who must be Dax, shifts disposition so quickly that it nearly gives me whiplash as he lowers his fist and sinks to the ground, hugging the girl with the muzzle. That's when I remember. Her tattoo. DAX001. She belongs to him.

At first, the thought makes horror wash through me, knowing that she's stuck with someone as cruel as this man must be since he's part of this place. But as I watch Dax hold her, checking if she's okay, asking if Dorin hurt her, it's clear he cares deeply for her. I remember the almost peaceful look on her face when she showed me the tattoo—the anger when I thought it was a product of abuse. I have no idea how this man got her to want him or what illicit methods he used, and as I watch her sink into him, I think it doesn't matter. Despite the brutal nature of this place, she's in a much better place than I've been for years, protected and cared for, safe from other men and their brutal intentions.

I flinch as Dorin returns to me. I expect his face to remain icy with menacing fury, but as I chance a glance up at him, his features are back to the usual impassive expression. He grabs my face again, this time gently, and studies it.

"Are you okay? What did she do to upset you."

"No-nothing," I stammer, the shaking in my body seeping into my voice.

He detaches the straitjacket from the wall and watches me with inspecting eyes as he sweeps my hair off my shoulder, checking my neck, my head, and my face. My world rattles as he cradles my face between two strong hands and bends his knees to come to my level as he searches my eyes. His expression remains stiff and hard, but deep within his cold gaze, there's a fierce protectiveness that makes me want to crumble and sink into him. I can't, though.

Averting my gaze, I tighten my muscles as I struggle to shut him out. When he brushes his knuckles over my cheek, I nearly break. It hurts to reject him like this, but I need to withstand his warped care. No matter how badly I want it. Because I know nothing good will come of it. No matter how obsessed or possessive he is, it doesn't change the fact that he's going to sell me in the end.

23

DORIN

"She needs to be punished," I demand as I turn away from Lavinia, aiming my attention at Dax's girl. "By me." I unclip my baton from my belt, itching to use it on that little bitch for making *my* girl cry. *Fucking Dax*, letting his sub scurry the halls and do whatever she pleases. I want to punish Dax too for being so reckless, but I know that's not going to happen, so teaching that little bitch a lesson will have to do.

Dax darts off the floor. "The hell she does." He's coming straight for me again, but Mikhail steps in, stopping him with a hand on his chest. I grind my teeth in frustration. I would have loved to slam my fist into Dax's face.

"What happened here?" Mikhail demands, always meddling in other people's business.

Tightening my fist around my baton, I point at the bitch cowering against the wall. "She bothered my girl. Made her cry."

"Why was she here in the first place?" Mikhail asks.

"To harass my girl."

"Dax?" Mikhail ignores my answer and turns to Dax

instead. I damn near take the moment to rush across the hall and wield the punishment that needs to be doled out.

"If Dorin didn't bring her here, I have no clue." Dax turns to his girl before I can go through with it, which is probably a good thing. I need this place, and as much as Mikhail tolerates my occasional fuck-up, this clearly would be crossing a hard line. "Did you walk off?" Dax asks her.

She gives the tiniest nod, and I scoff. I thought Dax just let her wander about, but it seems he has no clue what she's up to—he can't control her.

"See, she has to be punished," I tell Dax, stating the obvious. "Since she bothered my girl, it's only fair that she gets it from me. If you want to have a go at her too, be my guest and continue once I'm done."

"No, Dorin," Lavinia begs behind me. "It's not her fault. She tried to help me."

"She fucking went to you without permission. She gets punished," I tell her, then aim my attention at the girl about to taste my stick. "You'll learn your lesson hard."

I regret having released Lavinia from the wall as she scurries across the floor and presses herself into me. "No, Dorin. If anyone has to be punished, punish me. I'll take it for her."

I push her aside. She probably hopes I'll kill her with my stick, and it goddamn infuriates me, making me want to punish her too.

"Please, Dorin. Let me take it," she begs again, just like she begged me to let her take her own life in the tub a week ago. I'm about to either bark at her or take the syringe in my pocket and snuff out those infuriating suicidal thoughts with drugs, but Mikhail interrupts before I can decide.

"Silence! I'm sick of this. You two clearly aren't capable of figuring this out yourselves, so I decide who gets to punish who."

My blood boils as I watch Mikhail. I think I just might rip his head straight off his body if he makes the wrong decision. But then again, it probably wouldn't be such a good idea. Dax would probably be the fucker to take over this place, and there's no way in hell I'm going to take orders from an idiot who can't even keep a girl under control. So I accept Mikhail's decision and await his decree. Which is fucking ridiculous.

Pointing at my songbird, he says, "She gets the punishment." He points at Dax's girl. "She gets to watch."

I'm about to protest, but Mikhail stops me. "I don't have time for this. Get on with the punishment, or I'll hand your special little project off to someone else." With that, he walks away.

I gnash down on my teeth, but when I turn to see the relieved expression on my songbird's face, my anger gets a new target. As much as I want to punish Dax's girl, I want to make *her* hurt. For wanting to leave me so fucking badly.

I grab her by the arm and steer her down the hall. Leaning in, I snarl into her ear, "Don't even think for one second that I'm gonna beat you to death. I know just how to wield this stick to make it *hurt* without causing any lasting damage."

She gasps. "That's not—"

"Shut up." I don't want to hear any of her fucking excuses.

She remains quiet as she stiffly follows along, wobbling beside me and almost falling several times as she struggles to keep up with my long strides, still dazed from the drugs lingering in her system.

She doesn't protest as I lead her into a whipping room and place her beneath the ceiling hook we use to string up girls. Her compliance only angers me further. I have no idea what's going through her mind, but I'm sure it has to do with some kind of warped hope that I'll end up beating her to death. Or maybe it's like a twisted sort of self-harm to escape—me. The need to punish her for hating me and wanting to leave so damn badly blots out my need to punish the other girl, and I barely even notice that Dax walks in behind me with her.

"Stay," I tell her as I go to retrieve a bundle of ropes from the wall. When I get back, she's in the exact same spot, staring stiffly at the wall as I come up beside her and start unbuckling the straitjacket.

"Are you still hoping I'll beat you to death?" I ask as I help her out of the sleeves.

She gives a slight shake of her head, jaw clenched tight as she refuses to meet my gaze.

"Good." I don't know if she's lying or if it's dawning on her that she's about to feel the full brunt of my anger without getting the release of death at the end. Something is getting to her, that's for sure. She starts shuddering as I wrap the ropes around her wrists, lift them into the air, and attach them to the hook.

Frantic whimpers erupt from behind me, from Dax's girl, as I unclip my baton from my belt. A small surge of satisfaction rushes through me knowing she, too, will get some kind of punishment just by witnessing my brutality.

My blood swooshes through my veins as I feel the heavy weight of the baton in my hand. The chaos in my mind dwindles to a low simmer as I bounce it in my palm, grip it tightly, and aim. Everything around me disappears in a vacuum as I strike.

The baton thuds against her ass, hard and unforgiving. She jerks under the force, but there's nothing she can do. She's mine to abuse. Mine to hurt. Power swells inside me. A heady feeling that's close to soaring. I strike again. Her right thigh. Her left thigh. Her knees briefly cave in, and I feel strong and mighty. In control.

But something's off, I realize, as I lift the stick to strike again. There's no scream. No frantic writhing. She just stands there. Taking it.

The girl behind me screams, though, like she's the one receiving the blows. It's a good thing Dax has her wearing a muzzle, or I'd have to beat her for making so much noise and distracting me.

I take a step back to put in more force, and that's when I notice the whole picture in front of me. Her scarred back. The cuts, the burns. Her blonde hair spilling over her milky skin. Then mental visions flood my brain. The blood in the tub. Her vulnerable eyes staring up at me, begging me to end it all. The sound of her song in my ears.

I fling the baton aside, and it clatters against the wall across the room. The baton is for breaking; this girl is already broken.

Then I do something I never do. I open my hand and aim my flat palm at her ass. On the rare occasion I use my hands, it's closed fists. I don't think I've ever spanked a woman. It somehow seems too merciful—too personal. But as I slam my palm onto her ass, it's like finding a glove that's a perfect fit. It's not as much the physical sensation of my palm around an ass. It's the feeling of her skin. Her body. This broken little creature that gives in to me in ways no one ever has before. Or did.

The force of my hand sends her forward, her feet scraping against the rough floor as she staggers to regain balance, her wrists straining against the ropes that catch her. I can't have that. She only gets the bruises I allow. So I press my left palm to her upper stomach, just below her breasts, supporting her as I deliver another heavy blow of my hand. This time, a tiny yelp escapes her. I almost miss it as the sharp sound of the smack bounces off the walls. Pulling her closer, I lean in to listen as I deliver another blow. Sure enough, there's that tiny sound again. It's despair, grief, and helplessness all wrapped in one small, but potent package. I wrap my arm around her waist and lean my head against her shoulder, needing to comfort her even as I deliver two more staggering smacks that has her chest shuddering.

"That's it," I whisper, pressing a kiss to her temple. "I've got you."

Suddenly, she starts shaking, all over. It's like a small but violent storm that rips through her and threatens to tear her apart. But I won't allow that. I hold her together as I deliver two more blows.

"Ah," she cries this time, collapsing into me.

"I've got you," I repeat with a sincerity that takes me aback. I want to hurt her—I crave her screams and her trembling desperation—but I want to comfort her just as much. It doesn't make sense, but it doesn't have to. I let myself drift away with the current, offering her more words of comfort even as I rip her world to shreds. "I'll protect you." *Smack! Smack!*

Finally, she screams.

I hold her closer. "You're mine. I'll kill every man who even tries to put his hands on you." *Smack! Smack!*

Her scream is full of an agony so deep it digs into my bones and makes me shudder. "I'm the only one who gets to have your pain." *Smack! Smack!* "Your screams." *Smack! Smack!*

Her chest shakes as she's on the verge of breaking down, but she's still holding back.

Grabbing her face, I demand her attention on me. Squeezing her eyes shut, she denies me what's mine to take, but I know it will come. I feel it in the air. She's about to give in; she just needs a tiny push.

"Look at me, my little songbird," I say, the softness of my voice feeling very strange but so right amidst the storm of violence I'm unleashing.

Her brows twitch a couple of times, her parted lips trembling as she struggles with herself. "I-I—"

Pressing a finger to her lips, I say, "No need to speak, just open your eyes."

Finally, she does. Her wide blue orbs are the

prettiest thing I've ever seen as her eyelids lift and she stares up at me with pain and vulnerability written deep inside them. The moment she sees me, her voice breaks. A sob escapes her, and she collapses, pressing herself into me with a fierceness I haven't experienced in her before.

Cupping the back of her head, I lean in to whisper against her ear. "Do you want me to stop?" I have no idea why I'm asking, but I know I'd stop if she asked me to. I'd take her down and carry her back to her cell right this moment if she said yes. But what she says instead bores straight into my heart and rearranges the whole damn organ.

"Just hold me," she begs, weeping into my chest. "Please just hold me."

"I'll hold you." Wrapping my arm around her waist, I hold her close as I place my hand on her ass again. "I'll hold you," I promise, placing a kiss on top of her head just before I lift my hand and slam it onto her delicate flesh two times in rapid succession. "I'll take care of you." I deliver two more smacks that have her knees buckling. For a moment, she just hangs there, her legs limp as she lets me be the only thing holding her up. Wrapping both arms around her, I relish every moment of it—her despair, her tears, her trust, and her sweet, sweet surrender.

When she finds her strength and her footing again, I move my hand back to her ass. Just as I'm about to strike, the strangest words I've ever heard leave her lips. "Thank you," she whispers.

Her voice breaks into a deep, grief-ridden sob as I

deliver two more blows.

I want to pause and ask why, but I don't want to break the trance. I give her a moment to recover before delivering two more blows. Two more. And two more. When she collapses again and can barely seem to support herself once she tries, I decide she's had enough. *I've* had enough. Every sob and shake racking through her body radiates straight into me, becoming my own. Suddenly, I feel exhausted. Overcome by a flood of emotions I can't grasp. I just want to hold her.

With one arm tight around her, I reach up to loosen the ropes with the other. Then I hoist her into my arms and carry her out of the room.

"Thank you," she says again as she burrows her head into my shoulder.

24

LAVINIA

The exhaustion and grief must have knocked me out when Dorin took me down and carried me through the halls, because I don't remember getting back to my cell. I also don't remember Dorin lying down behind me, hugging me close, and draping the blanket over us.

I lie completely still as I feel the wide expanse of his chest rising and falling in calm motions against my back. I'm not sure if he's sleeping or just resting, but feeling him this calm and relaxed against me is almost shocking. I can't figure out whether I like it—if I should melt into him or push out of his hold.

I *should* break away from this beast of a man, but the thought of losing his safe embrace tightens my chest, drawing the grief straight back toward the surface, threatening to crash me into despair. My chest stutters, my breathing coming hard, as I struggle to hold it in.

His fingers start moving against my arm, the tips softly caressing my skin, revealing he's awake. That soft comfort breaks whatever resolve or resistance I might have been able to salvage—just like his tender kiss did when he punished me.

I sink into him. I can't help myself. It doesn't matter what he's done or what he's going to do; I've missed him so damn much. His touch, his comfort, even his brutality.

It *hurt* when he punished me. Those first three strikes with his baton nearly broke me. I thought my mind was about to cave in and I'd never be the same again. But then he threw it away and pulled me close while he spanked me, and the resistance I'd held on to for so long started crumbling. That combination of his cruelty and comfort did me in, but not in that devastating, irrevocable way. It was in that same way as when he stole my dignity with the straitjacket, the gag, and the dildo, or the electrotherapy. It freed my mind and my emotions, allowing me to cry it all out in the safe space of his embrace.

A small whimper escapes me at all the conflicting emotions those memories give rise to. In response, Dorin tightens his grip protectively and presses a soft kiss to my shoulder. It's that same tender kiss he gave me when he punished me, so full of affection and care.

I sink into him, my resistance slipping away like a boat being carried by a strong current. This is the best feeling I've had since that guard came in here and shattered my world and the blissful illusion I was living. I've been miserable ever since, and I know I will be again, but right now, I'm not. I need to hold on to that for as long as I can, because this might be my last chance to get it. It doesn't matter whether Dorin still intends to sell me, or if the punishment shifted something within him the same way it did me. I need this—his safe stability and freeing brutality—as long as I can get it.

"Why?" Dorin asks, breaking the silence with a soft whisper.

"Why what?" I croak, my voice hoarse from all the screaming and crying.

"Why did you thank me?"

Did I thank him? For a moment, I don't even remember. I search through the mental images of the punishment before I recall it.

The overwhelming gratitude comes rushing back with a clarity that has my chest shaking with a long inhale. I'm not sure why it's there. It doesn't make sense that I thanked him for the pain and brutality or the way he stripped down my self-control, but somehow, that's what stirs the gratitude. Because that pain broke me out of my shell. It was like a knife through the stiff barriers, tearing through my flesh but allowing the searing despair a way to escape. It created an entryway for his comfort to seep in and fill the barren emptiness on the inside. I don't know what it is about Dorin, but the way he delivers the pain and humiliation builds me up rather than tearing me down, unlike all the other pain I've suffered throughout my life.

"I don't know," I say, having no idea how to put those emotions into words. "For... hurting me."

Pressing a hand to my cheek, he turns my head to face him. The dim ceiling light casts a careful glow into our corner, lighting up the unmarred side of his face and leaving the scar in the shadows. He looks almost confused, maybe even vulnerable, as he searches my face for some kind of explanation.

"You shouldn't thank me," he finally says. "I destroy

everything I touch. I don't want to do that to you." Something about the way he says it makes it feel like it's the most honest, personal thing he's ever told me.

I just stare back at him for a while—his rough features, the hard look in his eyes, and the thick scar camouflaged by the shadows. He's evil and brutality incarnate. I believe it when he says he destroys everything. But not me. Somehow, he mends me. It's like when a negative times a negative equals a positive—his brokenness and mine, tangled together, somehow heal instead of harm.

"You're not destroying me," I say. "You're healing me."

His thick brows draw together in confusion. "I'm not. You want to die. So badly. I think you'd actually do it this time if I let you."

"That's not because of you." I swallow hard, wanting to throw all the blame on him. That would be the easiest thing to do and more than justified. But the way I got here stopped mattering long ago, before I even knew I was kidnapped. What truly broke me was that guard, the way he crushed the illusion and shattered my slowly mending hope. If Dorin had eased me into the truth, I might have coped somehow. I don't know. It doesn't matter. Dorin wasn't the one to truly break me.

He goes quiet for a while, deep in thought as his gaze goes distant.

"Do you still want me to kill you?" A scary shadow descends over his face as he focuses on me again. "To beat you to death with my baton?"

It's my turn to watch him with confusion. But then

realization strikes as I remember what he said when he dragged me off to be punished. "I didn't want you to beat me to death," I say in a weak voice.

He lifts his brows in disbelief.

"I didn't. I wanted to take the punishment so you wouldn't beat her. The girl with the mask." It doesn't mean I wouldn't have wanted to die, but that wasn't my motive in that very situation. The sweet escape of death didn't even cross my mind when I saw my only friend cowering and scared to death.

He gives a stuttered shake of his head. "You actually wanted to take the punishment for her? To spare her?"

I nod.

He roams his eyes over my face as if searching for a lie. "Why?"

That single word seems to say everything I've subconsciously suspected about Dorin but couldn't quite grasp. No one's ever loved him. Not truly. He doesn't know how to love. His comfort has been staggered and detached from the first time he held me. It's always felt sincere, but far from natural.

I shrug. "She's my friend. The only person who cares about me."

His jaw tightens at those last words, and I realize something else. It's yet another thing that doesn't add up, but it's evident in every comforting action and sweet caress: Dorin cares about me. On some warped level, he has found it in his cold, cruel heart to care for me. I don't know if it changes anything in the long run, but right now, it changes everything.

"I'm sorry," I say, biting my lower lip as guilt washes

through my fogged-over brain.

"For what?"

"For wanting to die on you."

A quick contraction makes him blink as an almost terrified expression flashes across his face. "Do you still want to die?"

"I don't know."

He doesn't say anything for a while. He absently strokes me as quietness descends and wraps us in a calm bubble. I'm about to drift off when he speaks again.

"I'll fix you." The confident determination in his voice is almost shocking as it breaks through the silence. "I don't know how, but I've done it before. I promise I will heal you this time too."

25

LAVINIA

"It's time for therapy," Dorin says when he comes into my cell sometime after breakfast the next day.

I stare at him with blank eyes, thinking I didn't hear right. But I did. His words were clear as day. "Therapy?" I finally manage.

"Therapy," he confirms. "I promised to make you feel better. This will help."

That's what he said the first time. But this time, I know it's not real therapy. I know how fucked up and wrong it is. I want to say that it won't help, but those words would feel like a lie. Because Dorin's fucked up brand of therapy has been all I've wanted since he stopped touching me—until someone else took me from my cell and touched me.

That guard who dragged me from my cell, caned me, and fucked my ass.

Suddenly, it's all I see, those ghastly memories. The room draws back yet closes in all at once, my vision blurs, and breathing becomes like heaving underwater. Words assault me, vile and malicious.

You're not so special now, are you? Just a dirty whore

getting used the way she deserves—fucked in your dirty little ass like a useless...

Squeezing my eyes shut, I cover my ears, but it does nothing to shut out the cruel voice. And then Zoltan is there too.

Beg me, bitch! Cry for me! Come for me, fucking slut!

"No, no, no," I pant, burrowing my head between my legs as the memories come rushing back with a vividness I haven't experienced in months. The horrible pain—the knife across my ribs, the cane ripping into my skin. The gut-wrenching humiliation as some stranger forced himself into me in an alley, or in a sordid dungeon room, or when I willingly let my abuser slide inside me and fuck me, all just for a little hope that always was hopeless.

I can't even remember who did what. It all blurs together. The faces, the voices, the pain, and the despair.

"Please, make it stop, just drug me again. Just kill me."

"Look at me," a voice demands, ripping into my despair.

"No." I can't face another man who wants to harm and humiliate me. I just can't.

Hands carefully grab my wrists and pull them from my face. "Look at me, Lavinia," the voice repeats. No *slut, whore,* or *bitch.*

"Please," I beg as I peel my eyes open and stare at another man who can easily force me into submission.

But as I watch him, it's neither terror nor despair I feel. Blinking rapidly, I flicker my gaze across the cruel scar, the rough features, and the hard eyes—the man more scary than any of the others. But most of all, the man who found me at my lowest and saved me. The man who breathed new life into me.

"Dorin," I whisper, my lips suddenly trembling. "I can't—I don't—" I drop my head, suddenly bone-tired.

He scoops me off the floor, into his arms, cradling me against his strong body. I burrow my head into his shoulder, and I keep it there as he carries me from the cell, down the halls, into a new room, and sets me down on some kind of table.

Carefully lifting my head, I look around. We're in the medical room—the one where he administered "electrotherapy"—and I'm in the strange gynecologist's chair. A shudder rolls through me, but I don't try to protest as Dorin presses me into the chair and starts strapping me in.

"I'll obey," I say weakly as he pulls a long strap over my chest. "You don't need to do that."

He pauses and looks at me with a solemn expression. "No, but you need it."

I give a slight shake of my head, not following.

"You need the helplessness to let go."

"I don—" I swallow the negation. Because I think he's right. No matter how much helplessness I've been subjected to, no matter how much it has destroyed me, it seems to be the only thing that will make me forget the pain. So I change my words. "I don't understand this."

"Neither do I." He grabs my hand to strap it into the wrist cuff at the side. He's silent as he goes about restraining my other wrist too and strapping my legs to the stirrups. Then he comes to stand at my side and looks into my eyes as he says, "Nothing has made sense since I found you in that tub." He grabs the bite block off the side table and holds it before my mouth. "Open up."

I stare at him as his words send a new wave of bewilderment through my mind, making me see things from Dorin's perspective. If those pictures of the toothless girl the guard showed me really was Dorin's doing, he is not a good man. If anything, he's a monster. Yet somehow, he's been protective and caring of me. I know he has felt this weird bond between us too.

I want to ask if he's ever felt like this with another girl here, but I'm not sure I want to know. A *yes* would only kill the comfort I'm finding in this connection. So I hold back the words and open my mouth.

He looks stunned for a moment as he stares at my parted lips, the way I'm readily obeying. Lifting his hand, he traces his thumb across my bottom lip and slowly leans down. His breath comes hard against my mouth as he hovers right in front of me. I gasp as he sweeps his tongue across my bottom lip. It's curious and careful in a way that makes me think he hasn't done much kissing in his life. I remember the first time he kissed me. It barely qualified as a kiss as he forced his mouth upon mine and invaded me with a ferocity that snuffed out my breath. But now, he takes his time, tasting my lips and testing my reactions as he licks the corners of my mouth. I mewl as a tickly sensation sends tiny shudders of pleasure through me. I don't try to reciprocate or deepen the connection into a kiss. I just lie there, lips parted, letting him test and try.

When he ventures into my mouth, it's awkward at

first as he licks my inner lips and my teeth. But when he finally dips in, connecting our lips and joining our tongues, it feels like two wires connecting, coming alive. I match his rhythm, moving my lips with his in perfect harmony. He growls as he pulls my lower lip into his mouth, giving it a quick bite. Then he's back in my mouth, exploring and tasting, twirling my tongue with his, claiming my mouth with a possession that has me panting and mewling.

When he pulls back, I feel slightly lost. He turns away, leaving my side, and it takes me a moment to realize he put the bite gag away, leaving my mouth free. Sitting on the chair between my legs, he turns his attention to the space between my legs and the items on the rolling table. I search his attention for a moment, but when I don't get it, I press my head into the chair, focusing on staying calm.

It gets harder by the second as I hear him moving objects and the crackle of latex gloves tells me he's about to start. Breathing through rounded lips, I manage to keep somewhat calm, but when he spreads my ass cheeks and a trickle of cold lube drops onto *that* hole, I crash.

"No," I gasp, shooting my head up. "Not there." I shriek as he presses a finger into the moisture, breaching that first barrier, invading my ass. Like *he* did. "No! Dorin, no. Not after what he—what happened."

He sinks in to the first knuckle, then lifts his eyes, boring them into me with undebatable demand. "I'm gonna erase that memory and give you a new one."

"It doesn't work like that. What if—" I squeeze my eyes shut, already feeling the panic drawing in and choking me, threatening to drag me into the black pit he just took me from. I shake my head as my tight throat cuts off my ability to speak.

Everything spirals as he starts advancing again.

A cruel laughter breaks into my mind, blaring like a shrill alarm, then horrible words spoken in a sleazy voice. *"Dorin won't want you after I've taken you here." Pain erupts in my ass as he tears at my tissues and forces the head of his cock inside. "It's all he cares about, breaking in your tight ass. Once I've done that, you'll hold no value to him. You'll be a tarnished little slut, good for nothing. He'll toss you aside to be sold."*

I keep shaking my head, harder and harder, my head hurting from the effort.

"He won't," I croak.

"Oh yes, he will. He's like a dog like that."

"Lavinia!" A sharp command breaks me out of the horrible memory. Snapping my eyes open, I stare at Dorin—the man who kidnapped me to be sold, the man who locked me up and lied to me. The man who is once again invading me against my will. I shouldn't want him. But as the memory of the pain and terror remains fresh in my brain, so does the memory of the mind-numbing terror at the thought of losing Dorin. I don't know if it's some kind of trauma bonding or Stockholm syndrome, but he's the only person who has made me feel alive and cared for since I lost everything.

So I cling to him. I lock my eyes onto his and soak up his every word. Because they're all I have—and somehow, everything I need.

"Lavinia," he says sharply again, and there's a fierce

possessiveness to his voice as he calls me by my name for the second time. "This hole is *mine.* Not Jan's, not yours. *Mine.* I want you to feel that every moment of every waking hour. So you'd better damn well stay with me as I claim it—and get that fucker out of your head."

I swallow hard, stunned by his ferocity, and nod.

"Good. Now, stay with me and notice how it actually feels. You've healed down here. It's only the tip of my finger. It doesn't hurt."

I heave a deep breath and turn my focus to my tight opening—his finger stuck inside.

"Am I right?" he asks.

"Yes," I say, the word coming out breathy. It feels strange and intrusive, but he's right. It's not painful.

He draws out and applies more lube. I inhale a sharp breath as the moisture runs down my crack in a cold trail. I fist my hands as he once again positions his finger.

"Mine," he says, holding my gaze in the demanding trap of his eyes as he pushes his finger back in.

I cling to his gaze as everything inside me twists wildly, about to spiral. I automatically clench my muscles tight to block the entrance, but Dorin easily sinks in to the second knuckle, invading me in the most horrible way I could imagine.

"This is my hole. Not Jan's, not yours. Say it."

"Uh, I—" I shudder as he advances further, and it takes everything I have to stay with him and not sink into myself and those horrible memories. "This... this hole is yours. N-not Jan's, not mine. Yours." As I say the words, something happens inside me. It's a strange well of emotion that builds and fills me to the brim. Tears pool in my eyes, and my whole world feels upside down, but not in a chaotic way. It's like my feet finally touch the ground after having been hanging with my head down for years. "I'm yours," I repeat, tasting and testing the words, soaking up that floaty sensation that grounds me and sets me free. "All yours."

"That's right." He sinks his finger all the way inside, then withdraws and positions two fingers at my opening. A smirk spreads across his features as he starts pushing against my tight ring of muscle. "*My* little songbird," he says with a grunt as he breaches my opening.

I gasp as my body gives in, opening up and letting him in. This time, he doesn't pause. He sinks straight in with one slow, steady advance. Blinking rapidly, I drift off for a moment, floaty and overcome by the intense emotions of belonging to this strong and dangerous man, who has somehow become my pillar of safety.

"Not Jan's, not yours," Dorin says as he pulls back out. "Only my hole to use."

The moment his fingers disappear, Jan slams back into my mind, poisoning the gentle stream. *It's all he cares about, breaking in your tight ass. Once I've done that, you'll hold no value to him.*

"Are you gonna leave me once you've taken me back there?" I blurt, suddenly gripped by the terror that I'll hold no value to him once he's reclaimed what Jan took from him.

Something feral deepens the dark pits of Dorin's eyes as he gets up and rounds the table. His movements are slow and deadly as he wraps his hand around my neck and leans in. "Once I've claimed you down there, you're *mine.* I'll want to be inside you over and over, feeling those tight sweet walls clench me, begging to be defiled—begging for *my* cock. You won't be able to get rid of me. I hope you'll be able to live with that because you're not getting away now."

I melt into the seat as I stare up at him, open and ready for him to claim every last cell and particle of my broken being.

26

DORIN

I had planned on using a probe in Lavinia's ass—not fucking her back there. But the way she's watching me, as if I truly am her whole world, like she *wants* me to claim her like that, changes everything. No one's ever wanted me down there, or in any other hole for that matter. But this girl does. She *needs* my brutality, and I need to possess her in a way I've never wanted to have anything in my whole life. All I've ever wanted was to destroy, but now, I want to claim and mend. I have no idea how, but with this girl, it seems I can do both at once.

Instead of taking the anal probe, I grab the other one and press it against her sweet little pussy. She's already soaked. I don't think she's even realized how horny she's gotten from having my fingers inside her ass. Her eyes go wide and surprised as I push the probe through her slickness and straight to the hilt.

"You like this? You like being a horny little slut for me."

Her mouth falls open. I think she's about to protest by the shocked look in her eyes. Instead, a low "Yes" falls past her lips.

I smile. "You're the most perfect little slut, and you'll be even more perfect once you have my cock inside that tight little hole of yours, screaming as I fuck and zap you."

Fear tightens her delicate features, but she makes no move to protest as I grab the lube, squeeze a generous amount onto her ass, and take out my rock-hard cock. She doesn't even flinch as I press it into the slickness. She just keeps staring up at me, letting me probe and prod against her opening. Slowly, her tense muscles relax, and tiny moans slip past her lips as I glide my cock through the lube, circling her opening. I guess she must be more sensitive down there than I expected. I keep going for a little while, drawing out her lust until her cheeks are flushed with a sweet deep red.

"It's time," I say, positioning my cock against her hole and pressing. "Relax for me and let me in."

Her brow tightens, her muscles tensing. But then acceptance slips in. She draws a deep, shuddery breath, and on her exhale, she releases all the fear and tension, opening up to me.

"That's it," I grunt as I press the tip inside. Digging my fingers into her thighs, I shut my eyes for a moment. This feeling is heaven. I've never taken my time to savor that first breach. Once my dick gets involved, I want straight in. But this first taste of what's to come sends a ripple of shudders and shivers through me that makes my skin hum all over and my balls twitch with delicious electricity.

Lavinia is still watching me, lips slightly parted, eyes

round and mesmerized, as I look at her again. The sight sends a buzz through me that has me shivering with a burst of pleasure. But as much as I enjoy seeing her peaceful surrender, I want to hear her scream too. Because that will make her surrender that much sweeter when she gives in again.

Grabbing the remote, I pierce her with a sharp stare that locks her in place and draws new fear to her features.

I press the button—medium voltage—and groan as she convulses, her muscles closing tight around me. Her eyes snap shut, her whole face tightening with pain, jaw clenched tight. She looks like she's about to either burst or draw in on herself, and I wait for a curious moment to see what will happen. What she does is nothing like what I expected. Peeling her eyes open, she stares at me with soft vulnerability, her muscles slackening in one smooth motion, like a gust of wind blowing through her body.

"Thank you," she whispers.

I just stare at her for a full minute, not comprehending what's happening, not knowing whether I'm dreaming. Finally, I move a little, pushing a little farther in. The tight feeling is amazing, but what has my balls drawing up is the way she opens up to me—body and soul. She keeps watching me as I advance, tiny moans slipping from her lips as I sink deeper into her tight opening.

"Why did you thank me?" I ask as I pause again to let her adjust.

Her shoulders draw up, her lips parting and closing. "For setting me free."

I hum at that. I know exactly what she means. Being here, inside her, seeing her openly succumb to me clears my brain and takes me away from all the cruel memories I've never been able to escape. Now, with her, they're gone. They're not even buzzing in the background, threatening to jump back the moment I rein in my brutality. It's just her.

"Ask me to zap you again," I say, finding that I don't want to force out her pain. I want to give it to her because she wants it.

"Please zap me," she says without hesitation.

A smile spreads across my lips as I turn up the voltage and press the button.

"Ah!" she cries, straining against the leather belts as the electricity rips into her body. Sweat beads on her brow, and her breaths grow staggered. Her eyes are slightly glassy when she opens them again. She struggles to focus on me, but I can tell she needs the connection, and I revel in it.

"Ask me again."

She blinks rapidly, then stares at me with wide, vulnerable eyes. "P-please, Dorin. Zap me again. I-I need you."

Shit. I nearly come at those words. Holding still, I suppress the orgasm. I want to draw this out.

"Please," she says again when I don't zap her. "Please hurt m—" Her plea morphs into a scream as I press the button. Her muscles contract and pulse around me, and I growl as I once again fight off the oncoming rush of sensation that threatens to throw me over. I need to get inside her quickly because I'm not ending this before she's taken my full length—before I've claimed her and erased every last trace of Jan and his filthy cock. I wish I would have kept him alive so I could cut it off and feed it to him.

I watch in awe as Lavinia comes out of the pain and stares up at me with slightly parted lips, tiny moans spilling from them as need takes over. "P-please take me."

"If you want my cock, you need to relax down here." I grunt as her muscles keep squeezing me, sending currents of pleasure through my nerves but making any further advance difficult without ripping her. She's so goddamn tight, and my girth is wide.

She closes her eyes, breathing through rounded lips as she focuses on relaxing.

"That's it," I tell her as she opens up. I push slowly but steadily, and her breaths come faster and heavier as I claim her ass. I think she's enjoying it, but when a pained whimper escapes her and her brows draw tight, I lean in and grab her jaw. "Look at me," I demand.

Her eyes fly open, and relief softens her features as I once again pull her out of the gruesome memories.

"Stay with me. *I'm* the one who's deep inside your ass. *I'm* the one you goddamn belong to. Are we clear?"

She gives me a tiny nod, and a long, deep moan flows from deep within her belly as I start moving within her.

"Ask me for more pain," I say.

She doesn't hesitate. "Hurt me, Dorin. Please make it hurt."

A smile draws up my lips as I turn up the voltage.

"With pleasure."

Her scream rips through the room, sending a shudder through me and making my balls draw up tight. I'm right at the edge and won't be able to hold for long, but I want her with me. I spit on her clit and press my thumb into the moisture, holding my cock still inside her.

"You have one minute to come. If you don't, you'll get the highest voltage."

Her eyes go terrified as she stares between me and the remote in my hand. "No, no, no," she begs, but the fear does the exact thing I need it to. Even as terror keeps her eyes wide, her moans lengthen, and the red hue in her cheeks deepens.

Her hips strain against the restraints, seeking more of my touch, trying to move around my cock. But Dax has made this table well. All she manages are tiny jerks. It's almost enough to throw me over, though.

"Time's almost up," I say even though only half a minute has passed. "Last chance." I hold up the remote, turning the button as she watches, head shaking as terror furrows her delicate brows. I start moving inside her, and her begging becomes a rising staccato rhythm of moans as she nears the peak.

"No. No. No. No."

Lowering the remote out of her sight, I turn the voltage down, and just as her muscles start to contract with her onsetting orgasm, I press the button.

She strains and convulses, jerking against the straps as her body becomes a battleground of pain and pleasure. Her delicious screams and moans fill the room, and her eyes roll back as she comes apart. I growl as I slam into her, fucking her wildly as her pulsing muscles milk my cock.

"Fuck," I say as the pleasure keeps shooting into my nerves, making me jerk wildly as I come inside her. "You feel so fucking good. All mine."

* * *

Lavinia is barely cognizant when I carry her back to her cell.

She barely moved as I freed her from the table, but despite her lethargic muscles, she wrapped her arms around my neck when I scooped her up.

I can't believe she's clinging to me, seeking my touch and comfort. I can't believe I *want* to comfort her. Everything is upside down with Lavinia, and even having been aware of that from the start, it has made me fuck up repeatedly. I've been so set on not tarnishing her that I've kept her broken. Because this girl doesn't need light to shine, I realize as I place her on the mattress and watch the peaceful look on her face as she blinks up at me, a soft smile curving her lips. She needs the darkness I can offer—like a bright star that can only be seen on a dark night sky. I felt it the first time I shot electricity through her body, I felt it the first time I locked her in the straitjacket and forced her to come, and I felt it when I punished her. Today, she even begged me for the pain. But not because she wanted to die or to escape. She wanted it to feel alive. Somehow, she finds peace in my brutality.

And I find peace in her.

I lie down behind her and drape the blankets over us, pulling her into my embrace and enjoying the perfect fit as she molds herself into my body. The tearing and the tarnishing are always what has made me feel strong and powerful, but as I lie here, feeling her open up to me, calm and peaceful despite everything, I feel a surge of power I've never felt before. Because I did this. I have the power to heal her.

27

LAVINIA

I settle into a new routine that kindles my hope anew and drowns out the horrible things I learned at the hands of the guard—Jan—who raped me.

Slowly, I heal from the assault. Knowing that Dorin kidnapped me and is keeping me captive hasn't changed the way my body reacts to him and his dark ministrations. Electrotherapy becomes a regular occurrence, and Dorin takes me back to the punishment room several times to string me up and spank me, then fuck my ass. The first few times he ties me to the hook in the ceiling—the same way Jan did—I nearly panic. But as with the electrotherapy, Dorin demands my attention on him at all times, thus slowly shoving the vile memories of Jan out of my head.

Dorin doesn't use his baton on me again, even though it's always hanging from his belt now. He only uses his hands. They're more than plenty to rip loud screams out of me and send burning pain into my flesh. He doesn't hold back—not with the forceful smacks, but also not the comfort. He'll wrap an arm around my waist and pull me into his body, holding me tight, as he rains heavy blows down on my ass. Sometimes, I scream and writhe, trying to evade the pain, and some days, I sink into him, accepting it openly. No matter how it starts, it always ends the same way—with me weeping in Dorin's arms, crying out the hurt and anger that has festered inside me.

Dorin even starts taking me to a workout room, where he drills me on the treadmill until my legs ache and I'm begging for a pause. The first few times, it doesn't take long to reach that point. Having been confined to a small cell for weeks, maybe even months, my body is weak and tired, but despite the slow progress, the exercise works wonders on both my mind and body.

I find myself growing more and more attached to Dorin, and I feel him doing the same with me. But no matter how much affection he shows me, I can't shake an ominous feeling gnawing deep in my gut. Deep down, I know there's no good end to this. I try not to think too much about it, but one day when we're lying in my cell after electrotherapy, Dorin asks a question that opens the gate to a well of worry and fearful questions.

"Do you still want to die?"

I consider it for a few quiet minutes. I have barely even thought about it for a long time.

Dorin has breathed new hope into me. He has sparked a desire that blooms and grows and craves more of the warped brand of pain and protection he offers. He has shown me that there's more to life than the struggle to stay alive.

Sinking deeper into him, I breathe in his scent and press my hands to his strong chest. "No," I say. *I want to stay with you.*

I don't dare to say those last words, afraid they'll ruin the moment as he hugs me closer and peppers tiny kisses onto my hair.

But as the quietness descends anew and my thoughts keep skipping down that dangerous lane, the anxiety grows, and I have to know.

"Do you still plan on selling me?"

I hold my breath as I wait for his response, the hope that he'll say no growing.

When he curves his wide palm around the back of my head and presses a long, tender kiss to my hair, I think he'll give me the answer I'm hoping for. But once again, everything comes crashing down—with one little word.

"Yes," he says.

My heart contracts, and a feverish rush of cold shudders through me. "What? Why?" I finally manage. "I thought—" I push out from him, needing some distance as he breaks my heart.

"That's why I brought you here," he explains, like it's a given.

My lips part and close as I try to say something, but a lump has lodged in my throat, blocking all sound. I thought things had changed. All those things he said and did... That I belong to him. That he'd protect me. I thought he wanted me.

Turning away from him, I wipe at my teary eyes as humiliation twists within my gut. I feel so damn stupid for thinking something had changed. I know why Dorin brought me here. I know he's not a good person. I know he's a lone wolf who thrives on pain and brutality. Yet somehow, I convinced myself that he could change for me.

He lifts his hand to stroke my hair, but I jerk away from him. Suddenly, I can't bear to be near him. It's too painful. "Then sell me," I say, fighting off the pressing tears. "Sell me or kill me."

"I can't kill you," he says, a grave tone making his voice deepen.

"Then sell me," I say, recklessly hoping it will push him to choose something entirely different that I almost don't dare hope for.

Regret tightens his voice. "I'm not ready."

"Then keep me," I say, holding my breath as I realize this has been my greatest wish for a long time. Maybe even before Jan crushed my world, and maybe even despite the betrayal I felt at Dorin afterwards.

"I can't."

"Why not?" I ask, even knowing it's useless.

"I don't know how." Confusion morphs into determination as he adds, "I don't want a girl."

"Not even me?" I shouldn't have asked the question, because the lump in my throat expands, and tears pool in my eyes as I turn and see the answer on his face. He doesn't say it out loud, but it's clear—at some point, he made the decision to be alone, and not even the bond that has grown between us can change that. *I* can't change that.

I want to cry. Sink into deep despair and let him mend the brokenness like he's done so many times before as I wept in his arms. But I can't do it. Not this time. Because this time, he's the one to have caused that bone-deep hurt. So I turn the hurt into anger.

"Then sell me," I snap, sitting up and scooting away from him. "Just fucking sell me."

He reaches for me, but I rip my arm out of his grip. "Sell me," I demand. "If you won't keep me, then get it over with."

He sits up too, and when he reaches for me again, I start hitting him. First, I only use my flat palms on his arms, but when he tries to pull me into him, I curl them into fists and bang away at his chest.

"Just sell me, goddammit. If you don't want me, then get rid of me."

He doesn't say anything. He just sits there, taking my banging fists until I wear myself out and break down, fat tears rolling down my cheeks as raw sobs claw at my throat. When I've worn myself out, too weak to resist his comfort, he pulls me into him. Then he just holds me. It's strange, though, there seems to be regret in his arms as he grabs me so tightly my breathing becomes labored. It makes the hope flicker back on, but the light is faint. And as Dorin remains quiet, showing no signs whatsoever of changing his mind, I can't take it anymore.

"Sell me," I say with determination.

Dorin inhales deeply, and his breath shudders as he pushes the air back out. It's almost like he can't stand the idea. But when he grabs my shoulders and holds me out to look at me, his gaze is emotionless—resigned. I have to look away quickly because it's too painful seeing him, hoping and wanting, and having that hope crushed.

"Are you sure this is what you want?"

"Yes."

He looks off to the side, his jaw clicking as he seems to consider something. When he looks back at me, there's a strange sort of hope in his eyes. "I'll keep you for a while. You can stay here, like you do now. I'll take care of you and protect you until I find a good buyer. Someone who will be merciful."

"How long will that take?" I ask, my voice straining with a new well of grief. *For a while.* That's all I get.

"I don't know. A few months. Maybe a year."

I shake my head with hopelessness. "I—No. It's too long." I pull away from him, jerking back when he tries to touch me again. "I can't bear it. It hurts too much. Just get it over with."

"Are you sure?"

"Yes. Sell me. Now. I can't be around you anymore."

His jaw tightens, and something dark settles over his features. He looks me up and down, then says, "Okay. I'll put you on tonight's auction. I'll come get you in a few hours to get you ready."

My throat tightens, every nerve in my body feeling raw and exposed at the mere proximity to him—aching for him and knowing he doesn't want me. "No. I can't do this anymore. Send someone else. I can't be around you. I just—" My voice breaks. "I can't."

The darkness in his eyes deepens, turning his pupils into two black pits.

It's almost like my rejection angers him. But before I can examine his expression further or respond, he turns his back to me. A sharp ache spears through my bones as I watch his big frame approach the door and I realize this will be the last time I see him. I want to rush up and grab him—say something. Give him one final hug. But the hurt is too deep. I just sit there and watch him go.

28

DORIN

I don't know what's happening to me as I leave Lavinia's cell. Anger coils tight in my muscles, and I feel out of control in a way that scares me. I need to get out of here, or I'll risk causing so much damage Mikhail will send me away for good.

On the way out of the dungeon, I pop my head into Dax's office, relieved to find him at his desk so I don't need to go looking for him, prolonging the risk of me fucking up beyond repair.

"I need you to add a girl to the auction tonight," I tell him.

"Which girl?"

"248101."

Dax lifts his brows in surprise. "Number one? The girl who sings?"

"Just do it," I snap, leaving the room before I break his nose for asking so many damn questions.

My blood pounds through my veins as I ascend the stairs to my quarters in the tower, taking two steps at a time. My adrenaline is spiking, violence crackling beneath my skin. I want to tear everything apart and burn this place to the ground. Ten years ago, I would have done it, but I've learned enough self-control and found ways to cope.

Not bothering to change, I whistle at Rex, who comes bouncing off the couch, ready to go out.

I spend three hours in the forest with him, running, walking, sitting on the edge of a cliff and staring out at the untamed wilderness. Then I run again, buzzing with new adrenaline and fury.

When I get back, I dump onto the couch, breathing hard. My fists clench and unclench as I stare around the room, imagining all the destruction I want to wreak.

I glance at the clock. Still five hours until the auction starts.

It's a late auction today. The buyers will start with a fancy dinner in the upstairs dining room, then free access to a few chosen girls in the dungeon before retreating to the auction room for drinks and a presentation of the girls that are up for sale.

I'm itching to go down to the fancy dining room and rip the throat of every last potential buyer that might end up leaving with Lavinia—hurting her and breaking her after I just healed her.

I consider doing it. But then what? I would be forced to leave this place, and Lavinia's fate would just be postponed.

I consider going down there and simply snatching her away and keeping her for myself. I could take her up here and tie her to my bed, keep her as my slave. Or maybe let her wander about in my quarters, cooking, watching TV, taking Rex for walks.

The idea lights a spark in a place inside me that has always been cold and barren.

I go to my bedroom and imagine her lying there, her blonde locks spilling over my pillow and her milky white skin draped in my comforter.

The image is beautiful and soothing, but as I imagine time passing—days, months, Lavinia growing used to her new freedom and getting to know more ugly parts of me—the peace shatters. Anxiety creeps in, crippling and clawing, tightening my chest and narrowing my windpipe.

Bringing her up here would give her a taste of freedom and normalcy—something she'll never get with me. That small taste would grow into something more, and she'd start to resent me for the things I do to her as the normal world came within her grasp. She'd turn on me and see me for the beast I am. Then she would hate me too, just like everyone else in my life always did.

Pressing my hands into the mattress, I lean forward as I suddenly can't breathe. My vision blurs, and a sharp pain tightens my chest. I wheeze through the constriction, thinking this is it for me.

Rex comes running, rubbing his head against my leg, whining.

I reach my hand back to touch his soft fur—the only creature who has ever stuck with me.

I drop to the floor, heaving through my tight chest as I press my head between my knees.

Rex keeps rubbing his head against me, and feeling him close helps calm me.

I'm not dying. It's just panic. I haven't experienced

panic this severe since I killed my father and freed myself.

I straighten, and my focus clears somewhat. *I need to get out of here.* I can't be here while she's getting sold, knowing I'm losing her.

29

LAVINIA

Time drags by at a horribly slow pace as I wait in my cell. When a guard comes to give me a toilet break, I inquire about the auction to know when it starts, but as usual, he doesn't speak to me.

Several hours seem to pass in stagnant, anxious loneliness. It's not until I've eaten my third meal of the day that a guard comes and takes me away to be prepared for the auction. He brings me to the medical room, where the biker-looking guy named Dax straps me into the same chair where Dorin has given me electro "therapy" so many times.

He waxes my legs, my pussy, and my armpits, then flushes out my bowels, using a big, needle-less syringe that he sticks inside my ass to fill my stomach with water. The whole process is not only painful, but humiliating in a way that scrapes away at my humanity. Even so, it doesn't compare to the aching grief lodged in my chest.

I thought I meant something to Dorin. All the possessive words and eager efforts to heal me. I thought he did it because he wanted me. But at the end of the day, I was only a curious project. A novelty to be explored until he lost interest.

When Dax is through with me, a guard comes to take me away again. He brings me to one of the rooms where they usually wash me. Instead of just letting me stand there, he strings me up by the arms, then hoses me down and washes me with a careless roughness I haven't experienced before—the first sign that I'm no longer under Dorin's protection. Next, he takes me to a dressing room with five other girls, who all look like they've been through a hell much worse than the one I've endured.

The guard points to a pile of lingerie and orders us to find something that fits, then makes us do our hair and make-up.

Two of the girls are trembling and fighting back tears, scared to the bone. The other three look numb—hollowed-out and broken, obeying on autopilot like robots.

I feel ungrateful as I watch them go through the motions that will surely bring them one step closer to their ultimate demise.

I shouldn't have asked Dorin to sell me. I'm not stupid; I know the men who will pay for women in a place like this are sadists and psychopaths. And now I'm about to end up at the exact same place I fled from a little over a year ago.

I should have accepted Dorin's offer to find me a good buyer. It would have been a luxury none of the other girls here would ever even get close to. But the thought of spending one more day with Dorin nearly makes me double over as a sharp pain tears through my insides. Tears press behind my eyes, and it takes everything I have to hold them in as I add a little make-up to my eyes and comb out my hair. Being around Dorin, knowing I can never belong to him is just too painful.

So this is the right choice. This way, I get out of the padded cell and get a chance to complete what I couldn't do the night Dorin found me. If I'm complacent with the man who buys me, or just acting numb and broken like the other girls, he won't think of me as a threat. I'll go along, and when the chance strikes, I'll end my own life.

Once we're all dressed and have done our hair and make-up, the guard herds us into a large room with red carpets on the floor, beautiful lavish paintings on the walls, and chandeliers in the ceiling. Old-fashioned couches, upholstered chairs, and side tables with decanters and crystal glasses line the sides of the room, leaving the center empty. Except for a raised podium.

I swallow hard as the guard herds us onto the long podium, his cane slicing through the air to snap at the girls who stumble in the impossibly high heels we're forced to wear.

Then we just stand there, no one daring to move a finger as we wait.

A little while later, men start filing in, a few at a time. They make themselves comfortable in the couches and chairs, chatting with each other while watching us hungrily, sipping amber liquor and red wine. Most of them are dressed in tailored suits, reeking affluence and old money. A few are wearing tracksuits, but their attitudes match the well-dressed men, their gazes cold and calculated, their postures arrogant and teeming with violence. They're just as rich, if not more, than the others, but just don't care to show it.

I'm trying not to think about who would be worse to be sold to when a cold, familiar voice breaks into my consciousness. As I turn my gaze toward the door, my world tilts and crashes.

Zoltan's charming, cruel smile sends a slash of pain across my ribs. My vision blackens as my memories take me straight back to that agonizing night when I left him.

I stagger in the tall heels as the earth shudders beneath me. A sharp lick of fire across my thigh makes me cry out.

"Stand still," the guard in front of me demands.

I rip my gaze away from Zoltan, gluing it to the podium, hoping he will somehow disappear. Hoping it was just a cruel mirage.

But there's no escaping this man. No mirage. He steps in front of me, and the sickeningly sweet scent of his cologne drags a wave of nausea up my throat.

"My, my, what do we have here?"

I don't meet Zoltan's eyes. I tell myself it's because I won't grant him the satisfaction, but really, it's because I'm spiraling. Seeing that vile smile of his again will make me crumble to the ground in a fit of panic.

"I'd like to place a bid," Zoltan says, gleeful victory rolling off him in thick waves.

Perforated brown oxfords, tailored slacks, and a black silk shirt appear before me as a man comes up beside him. "Let me get a chance to show you all the merchandise before we start bidding."

"I don't care about the others. I want this one."

Keeping my eyes on the ground, I see the yellow outline of a track suit as one of the other men comes up to the podium. I feel his eyes raking across me as if to find out what's so special about me.

"Five million," Zoltan offers.

The man who seems to be leading the auction considers for a moment. "Usually, I prefer to wait until I've presented all the girls and we start the biddings, but with this girl, I'm willing to make an exception."

The man in the tracksuit rounds the podium and watches me from behind. "Six million," he cuts in, just as the auctioneer is about to agree to Zoltan's offer.

"Ten," Zoltan counters.

"Twelve," the man behind me offers, and I sense he's only doing this for the power of competition.

"Thirty million," Zoltan says with finality. "I'll transfer the money immediately."

The man in the track suit grunts. "You're crazy. No bitch is worth that kind of money."

"Oh yes, this one is," Zoltan says to himself, taking a cigar from his inner pocket and lighting it. The puff of smoke elicits a sweet, cloying scent that sends me straight into a flashback of Zoltan pressing the burning butt onto my stomach—the searing pain as the embers melted my skin. I want to scream as the burn seems to crackle in every one of my round scars. It takes everything I have to remain upright.

"You have yourself a deal," the man beside Zoltan says. Throwing a quick glance up, I notice it's the same one who settled Dorin and Dax's argument about the punishment.

I'm trembling all over as the guard taps the cane against my ass, herding me off the podium. I nearly fall, but Zoltan grabs me by the arm, keeping me upright. It's a mercy I don't want. Icy shivers roll across my skin, nausea twisting in my belly. I want to pull away, but fear has me in a vise, stiff and frozen, only moving because I have to.

"Would you like any modifications to the girl?" the man in the black silk shirt asks. "We have a wide range of possibilities. Tattoos, piercings, tailored leather gear. I can get you a list if you'd like some inspiration."

Smoke puffs into the air as I feel Zoltan's eyes raking up and down me. "A tattoo doesn't sound like a bad idea," he muses. "Maybe even four. Yes, that's what we'll do. Four tattoos to make sure she never forgets who she is." His voice morphs into a snarl as he makes his decision.

"Perfect," the auctioneer says. "Let's go into my office to handle the transaction. Meanwhile, one of my guards will take the girl back to her cell, and one of my men will handle your request first thing in the morning."

"No," Zoltan interrupts, digging his fingers deep into my skin as a guard comes up to take me.

"If you want to test your new acquisition tonight, I can have her strung up in one of our fine whipping rooms, so you can have some fun before settling in for the night."

"I'm not leaving her out of my sight. I'm taking her home tonight. Get the tattoo artist ready now."

The auctioneer seems to be considering before he

takes his phone from his pocket and agrees. "I'll make it happen."

While he leaves the room with his phone to his ear, Zoltan takes a piece of paper and a pen from his inner pocket, casting cruel glances at me as he scribbles down two words.

"This"—he holds the paper up in front of me—"is the mark you'll bear for the rest of your miserable life. For as long as I allow you to live. Even if someone digs up your rotting corpse, they'll be able to see who you belong to."

I gulp as I read the two crude words. *Zoltan's whore.*

Sadistic glee makes Zoltan's eyes light up as he steps around me, pointing at one arm at a time, my stomach, and my upper back. "Here, here, here, and here," he says as he goes. "No matter where you look, you'll see what you are."

The world is spinning and black dots are creeping into my vision as the auctioneer returns. I barely register his words as he says, "My tattoo guy will be down shortly. Anton will take you to his office."

Zoltan grabs me with a bruising grip around my arm, hauling me down the corridors. I hold my head down all the while, focusing on keeping my feet moving.

Everything inside me withers as he leans in close and says, "I had just given up on finding you and decided to get a replacement the easy way. Who would have thought. There you were, as if brought to me by the gods."

My throat constricts, and I can't suppress a whimper as the corridors close in and terror darkens my vision.

"That's right, things are gonna get so much worse

for you than if you had stayed."

* * *

The guard leads us into the medical room and herds me into the gynecologist's chair with all the straps. Zoltan puts my legs into the stirrups and takes out his switchblade to cut off the lingerie. Then he spends five minutes toying with my pussy lips with the knife. I try to shut down and close in on myself, but Zoltan demands my attention on him.

"Look at me, slut," he demands, and I'm too scared to disobey. He lifts the knife to my stomach and drags the sharp tip across my flesh. "In a short while, my name will be embedded into your skin, making sure you'll never forget who you are. *My whore.*" He pauses. "Though, I could just carve the words into you instead." Resting the tip of the knife on my stomach, he holds his finger to the butt as he considers.

I don't move a muscle, don't dare to breathe as gravity pulls the tip into my skin, breaking it, making warm blood seep out.

Removing the knife, he focuses on me again. "No, a tattoo is much more clear, and I'll have plenty of chances to carve your skin later on." A wicked smile spreads across his immaculate features. Most people would find him handsome—I once did—but I see him for what he is now. A devil in disguise.

Zoltan turns as the door opens and Dax enters.

I nearly gasp when I see who he has with him. The girl with the muzzle. Despite everything, I manage a smile as she lifts her gaze from the floor. Dax makes her kneel on a pillow by the desk, and her brows knit with worry as she keeps lifting her gaze, glancing at me. I think she's supposed to keep her head down, but she can't quite manage as fear must be racking through her, knowing nothing good will come from the scenario unfolding before her. I can only imagine being in her place. I would be even more scared than I already am, knowing I was about to witness someone harm her without being able to do a thing about it.

"What do you want?" Dax asks Zoltan.

Zoltan hands him the paper with the crude words that I will carry to the grave. Closing my eyes, I heave a heavy sigh. I hoped to be able to die still belonging to myself. But what difference does it make? He's already marked my whole body, just not in words and ink, and I'll make sure he doesn't take my mind before I get the chance to kill myself.

Opening my eyes, I force all the horror and humiliation back and focus on the only thing that matters right now. *It's okay,* I mouth to my friend, wanting to reassure her. With her here, my fear for my own well-being has faded somewhat, the need to shelter her taking over.

She draws a heavy breath, her shoulders shaking as she exhales.

Closing my eyes softly, I give her a tiny nod to reinforce my silent words while Zoltan discusses the placement of the tattoos with Dax.

As I watch her sitting there, fearing for me—caring about me—I almost feel like everything will be okay.

Zoltan has always been reckless with his knives, letting them lie around, arrogant in his conviction that I wouldn't cause him any harm. I'm not sure if he'll be quite as stupid now, knowing he can't force my obedience with pretty promises and false hope anymore. But I'm sure he'll fuck up soon enough, and I'll get to reclaim what's mine—my life.

"You can go now," Dax says, making me draw a relieved breath that chases some of the tension from my bones. "I have what I need. She'll be ready for you in an hour or so."

Zoltan kills my relief immediately. "I'm staying."

"That's an extra five grand," Dax says as he starts preparing a tattoo gun.

"Fine," Zoltan agrees. Money never was an issue for him as long as he got his way. Moving to stand by my head, Zoltan grabs a fistful of my hair while Dax turns to finish preparing the gun. He seems to be keeping a close eye on the kneeling girl, who obediently keeps her head lowered as Dax faces her.

"Sit still," he tells her just before turning back to Zoltan and me. There's a slight hint of worry in his expression, and I wonder if it has something to do with his girl.

When he lifts the strap that goes over my stomach, Zoltan says, "No, I'll keep her still." Popping his switchblade open, he presses it to my throat. The edge grazes my skin with a warning that has me going achingly still.

"That's gonna cost you another five grand," Dax says, releasing the leather belt.

"Fuck no, I've already paid you people more than enough."

With a shrug, Dax grabs the strap again.

"Fine," Zoltan relents. "Five grand extra."

Dax steps back and turns to the side table, where he puts on gloves and prepares the ink. He pauses a few times to study the girl with the muzzle, and I sense him considering something.

He takes the tattoo gun, about to begin, but puts it back down and goes to the door. Sticking his head out, he calls out for someone to come and lend him a hand.

As Dax barks orders into the hall, Zoltan toys with the knife. He slides it down my chest and stomach. His arm is right at my face, his skin caressing my cheek with feigned intimacy as he moves the knife in a slow motion as if he's caressing me with it. As I stare at the blade, I realize this is my chance. The knife is not my enemy. It's my friend.

I act quickly, biting down on his arm. Hard. The bloody taste of copper filling my mouth and the feeling of flesh breaking under my teeth almost make me retch, but I bite deeper as Zoltan roars and tries to pull his arm away. It only takes a second for his hand to pop open and the knife to fall onto my stomach. It slides toward the floor, but I snap my hand out and grab it, not caring that I catch the blade and cut my palm in the process.

Before Zoltan can recover and snatch the knife from me, I scramble off the table and back up, pressing the knife to my wrist.

I can do it, I can do it, I can do it, I tell myself as I close my eyes and force all my strength into my hand.

And then I cut. The moment I pull at the knife, I know it's enough force to finally achieve what I was too much of a coward to finish before. But just as I pull, a hand clamps around my arm, yanking me back. The knife disappears from my skin, only making a shallow cut.

"No!" I cry out, pulling at my arm to try and cut again. "Let go," I demand, spinning around as I put in more force. I get it free, but the jerk sends my hand and the knife slicing through the air and cutting my assailer.

Or protector, I realize to my horror as I see the wide-eyed girl with the leather mask clutching at her stomach.

Her bleeding stomach.

I step back, shaking my head. "I'm sorry. I'm so sorry," is all I can say. I'd do anything not to hurt that girl, but in the process of hurting myself, I did it. *Why can't I just die?*

Chaos erupts around me as someone comes in. I keep watching her as Dax darts to her and takes her in his arms while someone pulls me back and wrests the knife from my hand. It takes a minute for me to realize that it's not Zoltan who has grabbed me, and a small gush of relief blows through me as I'm pulled out of the room, away from him. But the relief dies as my eyes flit back to the bleeding girl, who glances from her wound to me with shock and pain mixing in her wide eyes.

Regret unlike any curdles in my stomach as I think I just might end up killing her instead of me.

30

DORIN

I've been driving for two hours straight. It's well past midnight. By now, Lavinia is probably standing on the podium in the auction room while sleazy, stuck-up, arrogant men bid on her, wanting to get their filthy hands on her.

Rex makes a low whine from the backseat as I speed and hit a pothole in the gravelly mountain road, making the car bounce.

"Sorry," I mutter, reluctantly slowing down. I don't care about myself at this point, but I don't want to kill Rex. I have no idea why I even brought him or where we're going. Maybe part of me needed to bring him in case I decided not to return. It doesn't seem like such a bad idea. The thought of going back there and knowing she's gone is unbearable. Maybe I should just disappear deep into the mountains with Rex, build a small cabin, and stay there. He'd enjoy going hunting with me, and I might enjoy the solitude.

The thought swirls in my mind for another half hour, seeming more and more like a good idea.

When Rex starts whimpering and tapping his paw at

the window, I pull the car over at a wide place in the road and let him out to pee. Leaning against the car while waiting, I tap my fingers against my phone in my jeans. I'm itching to take it out and check the transaction logs to see if a sale on Lavinia has gone through, but I keep myself in check, knowing it will only make everything worse to see she's been sold.

"Good boy," I tell Rex when he returns from within the trees, bouncing with joy. I scratch him behind the ear, enjoying the way he leans into me. *This is all I need*, I tell myself. But as I let him into the back of the car and get into the driver's seat myself, I know it's not true. I need more. Leaning my head back into the seat, I close my eyes and conjure images of stringing a girl up and whipping her until she screams. But it's still not enough. The thought is nowhere near as satisfying as it used to be.

The image morphs. The unspecific girl takes shape. Blonde locks that fall in soft waves down her back. Long scars crisscross her milky skin. Old burn marks rise in uneven patches. Eyes as blue as a summer lake appear before my inner eye, watching me with trust and vulnerable surrender. I open and close my fist. What I wouldn't give to crash my palm onto the soft mounds of her ass, holding her close and soothing away the pain as she cries out. Comforting her and telling her everything will get better as the tears start falling.

I imagine bringing her upstairs, tucking her into my bed, and getting in behind her. Letting Rex join us and curl up next to her. Her petting his fur and me stroking her hair.

I breathe a deep sigh, finding a moment of contentment as I get lost in the idea.

But then time passes in my vision, just like when I thought about this earlier, and she comes to want more. She realizes what a monster I am, begs me to stop hurting other women, hating me because I won't—can't—change.

With a grunt, I open my eyes and turn the key to start the engine. It's a fantasy. It will never work in real life.

I'm about to pull off the side of the road, but I stop just as I'm about to hit the gas. Without thinking, I grab the phone from my pocket and log in to our system. Needing to know what'll happen to her, I check the latest sales. Whatever I find there won't change a thing, but I need to know.

I scroll down the list of sales for this week, almost not expecting to see her name since the sales probably won't have been finalized yet. But there she is. Her number appears at the bottom of the list.

Unit: 248101

Defeat settles heavily in my stomach. *It's done.* Now, she belongs to someone else, and soon, she'll be gone, out of my reach. I press the side button on my phone to put it back in my pocket, but just as the screen shuts off, I catch a glimpse of the buyer's name. Urgency rattles through me, stirring chaos into the acceptance and making my rage flare back alive with a vengeance.

It can't be.

Barely breathing, I turn on the screen again, and there it is, the one name I shouldn't see. The one name I *need* to see—the only one that will get me out of this ridiculous powerlessness, accepting her sale.

Buyer: Zoltan Stepanov.

I have been doing lots of research on this man during the last few weeks, planning and fantasizing about how to take him out, but postponing because I couldn't leave Lavinia. Now he's there. When I'm gone.

My blood curdles as horror infiltrates my brain.

Tossing my phone aside, I push down on the gas and pull the wheel hard, dragging up a cloud of dust as I make a hazardous turn.

"Sorry, Rex," I say as I speed down the bumpy road. "I need to get back. Fast."

31

LAVINIA

I'm back in the padded cell, strapped into the straitjacket, feet bound together. Helpless to the bone. Hating myself. Fear tightens my windpipe and makes black spots dance in my vision every so often as I go into a fit of panic. Fear for my own future and for the girl I hurt. My only friend, whom I might have killed.

I almost didn't care about the idea of going to a new man who'd torture me as badly as Zoltan did, or even worse. But the idea of going straight back into the claws of the monster I escaped makes me remember all too clearly just how horrible, mind-numbing, and soul-crushing that pain was. More so, it's a deep cut to my pride I can't live with.

At some point, the man with the perforated oxfords comes to check whether I'm hurt. I feel like cattle as he takes off the straitjacket and turns me to check my skin. A wide smile is plastered on his face. "I have no idea what's so special about you, first making Dorin act all strange and possessive—I actually thought he was going to keep you at one point. And now, a buyer bidding thirty million at first sight." He pats my cheek in a gesture that's more of a few soft slaps. "Thank you for making me a rich man." Pressing his hands to his thighs, he pushes up. "Well, even more rich." With that, he turns to the guard waiting at the door. "Get her back into the straitjacket. I don't want to have to do a partial refund if anything happens to her."

When he's about to leave, I break from my debased numbness. "Is she dead?"

He turns to me, a severe look making his already low brows draw lower, almost as if the girl means something to him too. "No."

Relief loosens the tightly coiled tension in my body, making me slump. I just sit there, staring into nothingness as the guard puts me back in the straitjacket, then leaves my cell and turns off the light.

I'm exhausted—tired to the bone—when the light comes on again and a new man enters. This time, it's the long-haired guy, who was supposed to mar my skin further with Zoltan's name. The man the masked girl sought shelter with. *Dax.*

"Are you here to take me to him? To Zoltan?" I ask, feeling dead inside.

"Not yet." He approaches me slowly, honing his sharp—no, murderous—attention on me.

Suddenly feeling like a maelstrom has ripped into my cell, about to tear me apart, I scoot away, into the corner. "Then why are you here?"

His lip twitches in a cruel expression as he leans down to snatch me by the hair. "To get my revenge."

Ice slithers through my veins, my stomach twisting with a foreboding feeling. I've sensed the murderous rage in Dorin when someone hurt me. I even saw him kill a man for harming me. Now, I'm the one who harmed the girl. I'm the one who will pay dearly.

Even knowing it's no use, I try to plead with him. "I'm sorry, I didn't mean t—"

Slamming his hand over my mouth, Dax whips me around and hoists me up with an arm around my waist.

Instinct takes over, and I kick and scream. But it's no use. I'm strapped in tight in the straitjacket, my feet bound, and Dax is as strong as Dorin. There's nothing I can do as he carries me off.

I'm certain I'm getting prepared for my execution as he straps me into the chair in the medical room. The idea that he's about to end me should please me, but for once, I don't want to die. All through the action, even seeing Zoltan, I've held on to the hope that Dorin will come for me. It's a stupid, naïve hope, but I can't let go of it.

"No," I cry out as straps tighten around my wrists, ankles, and stomach. "Don't do this. I'm so sorry." When my pleas don't work, I try something else. "Dorin will kill you for touching me."

At this, Dax laughs. Grabbing my chin, he leans in to spear me with a cruel gaze. "Dorin's not here now, is he? He doesn't care about you."

His words are like a stab to the heart. A stab that crushes my hope as I realize he's right. Dorin is not coming for me. He made his choice—tossed me aside to be claimed by the devil. I go slack, staring at the ceiling, welcoming death, as Dax uses several straps to fasten my head.

It's not until he straps my face in with pins and

metal fixtures as if I'm about to undergo head surgery that it dawns on me how strange this is. New fear surges through my veins. I strain against the straps and the pins, but they're too tight. All I can do is flit my eyes from one side of the room to the other.

"What are you doing?" I croak as he dons surgical gloves and disinfects my throat. Somehow, I just know he's not giving me the easy way out by killing me. He wouldn't go through all this trouble of strapping me in tight for that. Dax is going to make me suffer for what I did.

"Don't worry. I've done this to a lot of girls over the years. I even got a few to practice on before filling an order. Only one of the early ones died from complications. I'm very good at what I do. Unlike Dorin, I haven't cost Mikhail much merchandise loss."

A wicked smile gleams in his eyes as he lifts a syringe and aims it at my neck. "I really hate to sedate you for this, but too much muscle movement will heighten the risk of complications, and I want you to live to feel this."

I scream as the sharp needle sinks into my neck.

"That's right. This will be the last scream coming up your throat."

Terror becomes a thick haze over my brain as the sedative seeps in, stealing my scream, stealing my voice. All I can do as Dax sinks a scalpel into my neck is flit my eyes back and forth and sink my nails into the padded surface until they break.

32
DORIN

The first thing I do when I get back is to search for Zoltan. I have a nagging urge to go check on Lavinia in the padded cells, but I tell myself it's just out of habit. Chances are she won't be in her cell. If she's even here, she might be with Zoltan, and I'm not giving him a minute longer to hurt her.

Once again, nothing is like I thought it would be as I pick the lock on the suite assigned to Zoltan at four in the morning. Barging in, I find the room dark and the son of a bitch sleeping peacefully.

He sits up with a start. "What the hell are you doing in here?"

"Where is Lavinia?" I ask, watching him closely from across the room. I'm not making the same mistake as with Jan, killing him quickly. With this fucker, I'll take my time, make it slow and painful. He'll suffer ten times as much as Lavinia did at his hands.

"I should ask you the same thing." He stands up to face me straight on, arrogant and reckless in believing he has any say here—that he's safe. "I want her *now*." He shoots his finger toward the ground in a demanding gesture. "I paid a fortune, and then you idiots take her away. You'll lose so much business over this when I tell my contacts how unprofessional this place is."

I stalk toward him, and I almost laugh as it slowly dawns on him that he probably shouldn't speak to me like that. He remains in place, but I can tell it's a struggle as his chin goes higher and his posture goes unnaturally straight. This guy may think he's seeming all confident and powerful, but I can smell the fear rolling off him.

My cock stirs in my pants as I grab him by the throat and lift him into the air.

"What the hell are you doing," he demands, but his words come out wheezy, and his brave façade crumbles as I squeeze, allowing him only just enough air to remain conscious.

Panic makes his eyes go wild as he grabs on to my hands and digs his nails in. I grunt at the delicious sensation as he breaks my skin. It makes me feel alive, and my cock swells at the feeling of his desperate, futile struggle.

I hold him in the air for a minute, imagining his screams as I break in his ass and snuff out the last flicker of his pride. But I have lots of other things I want to do to him before that. First, I need to stow him away somewhere he can't escape, and then I need to go find Lavinia and feel her in my arms.

Releasing him, I deliver a punch to his face that knocks him out before he can find his footing. Then I fling him over my shoulder and carry him down to the dungeon, where I throw him into a cell. I strip him of the few clothes he's wearing, shove a butt plug up his ass, and chain him to the wall.

Finally, I make my way to the padded cells, relief calming the pumping adrenaline in my veins as I imagine having my songbird back in my arms. But something nags at me as I press my finger to the biometric scanner. Even as I open the door and see her lying on the mattress, I know something is wrong.

Her back is to me, and she's lying completely still. She's not in the straitjacket, and my memory flickers to the night I found her biting her arm, nearly killing herself with the sheer force of her teeth.

I rush to her, turning her, looking for blood. Looking for signs of life.

I don't find any blood, but I don't find much life either. Her chest is moving, her pulse beating, but her eyes are vacant. She doesn't even look at me, not even when I grab her chin to direct her attention to me. Her eyes remain unfocused, all hope—all life—gone.

"Lavinia." I give her a slight shake. "Say something. I'm here now. I'm not leaving you again. Not ever." I don't know what I'm saying; I have no idea how this will work. All I know is that I'm keeping her, no matter what.

"Say something," I repeat, shaking her a little harder when she doesn't react.

She swallows hard as if grief is lodged deep in her throat. It's only then that I notice the bandage. Right at her windpipe—her vocal cords.

Terror has my breath speeding as I grip the tape and rip the bandage off. The small, clean cut on her throat looks harmless compared to everything I've seen. But I instantly know what it is—who did this. Only one person here knows how to do the procedure.

Fury unlike any rises within me. My pulse hammers away as I lift Lavinia into my arms and hug her tightly.

"It's okay. I'm here now. I'm here for you. Anything you need, I'll give it to you." I close my eyes hard at those last words, knowing exactly what she'll want.

She sinks into me, her hands weakly grabbing on to my T-shirt. Relief takes the brunt of the anger boiling inside me. *She's not pushing me away.* She should, though. This is my fault. I'm the one who let this happen. I left her. I told Dax to put her on auction.

I did this.

My chest shakes as regret is about to get the better of me.

Grabbing Lavinia by the arms, I hold her out and aim my gaze straight at her. "He'll pay for this. Dax will pay. So will Zoltan. Anyone who ever hurt you will pay dearly. I promise you this."

* * *

After holding Lavinia for a long time and putting the straitjacket on her, I go to Dax's girl's cell. As expected, he has reset the biometric scanner. I'm not sure what I'm going to do to her once I get to her—because at some point, I will. But right now, I don't need to know. I'll enjoy making plans while biding my time. I can be patient when I want something enough. And I've never wanted anything as much as I want to get back at Dax for taking Lavinia's voice.

A stab of loss has me halting in my steps as I realize

I'm never going to hear her sing again. My chest tightens, and the world draws in. I'm about to have a goddamn panic attack again.

Refusing to succumb to that helplessness, I let my fury steer me on. I trudge to Dax's office, slam the door open, and bark, "What the fuck did you do?"

"What she had coming," he says with a calmness that is mostly fake, judging by the way he reaches for the gun in his waistband. *Fucking coward*, doesn't dare to take me on with his bare hands.

"You've fucking destroyed her. *My* girl!" I growl, tightening all my muscles to avoid going straight at him and risking getting shot. If it wasn't because Lavinia needs me now more than ever, I wouldn't care.

"She cut what belongs to me, so I cut something of hers. Eye for an eye and all that. You grew up catholic, right? So you'll understand."

And I killed the fucker who preached those words. I slam my fist into the cabinet beside the door, making a dent in the metal. "You won't see it coming, Dax." I'll fucking kill both him and his girl. I'll do her first, making him suffer for a while before I take him out. "You won't see it, but I promise you'll regret it."

I barge out again, slamming the door behind me. I itch to go back to Lavinia and hold her in my arms, but I'm afraid my furious energy will only scare her. There's no way to keep it hidden right now. So I do the only thing that makes sense with this fury raging inside me. I go upstairs, get Rex, and run into the woods.

I have no idea how long we spend among the trees and the mountains, running endlessly. Dawn is breaking when we get back, and I'm exhausted. I just want to collapse on my bed and sleep. But more so, I need to check on Lavinia.

She's still lying stiffly on her back, staring at the ceiling, looking dead.

Even knowing there's no way she can have taken her own life, I rush to her and check her pulse. The relief I find at the slow beat barely does anything to relieve the pressure bearing down on my chest, though. I can't remember ever being this scared, not even when my father held a broken bottle to my neck for the first time and I felt the warm trail of blood as the sharp spears penetrated my skin.

"Lavinia, please look at me." I wrap her head in my hands. "Just look at me."

No reaction.

I try a few more times, shaking her gently, begging her to watch me, but her eyes remain dead, her body unmoving.

With a heavy sigh, I give up, lift her up to sit, and take the straitjacket off her. I position her in front of me, draping an arm around her waist to hold her in place as I scoop up a spoonful of the good beef stew only the trainers and guards get.

"You need to eat," I tell her, holding the spoon to her mouth. But no matter how much I press and prod, she won't open. Finally, I give this up too and move down to lie on the mattress with her in my arms.

She's stiff and barely moving, but as I trail my fingers across her skin, rock her gently, and whisper soothing words, she loosens up. At first, it's only small twitches and shuddery breaths, then her chest starts shaking, and finally, the tears let loose. Raw, voiceless sobs form in her throat. The soundlessness only seems to intensify her grief to the point where she's jerking with the force of her sobs and her breaths come in small, shallow gasps.

"Look at me." I turn her around and grab her face between my hands. "Look at me, Lavinia."

Her eyes remain empty and unfocused, the seeping tears the only life. Nothing helps as I shake her, slap her softly, and keep urging her to look at me. It's like she's gone. Her eyes go cloudy as she keeps hyperventilating, and helplessness becomes a sickening twisting in my gut. I almost can't breathe as I keep watching her—the girl I want more than anything, but can't have. Coming back here, I felt hope for the future. I had no idea how things would work out—me with a girl—but it seemed right. Suddenly, I could see what I had been blind to ever since the first time I saw her. I *need* her.

But fate never was kind to me. Or maybe I'm the one killing it with my darkness like I do with everything. It doesn't matter. It's too late. Lavinia is gone, and as I look into those dead eyes again, I think I might not ever get her back.

33

DORIN

I spend the next few days watching over Lavinia, trying to get her to focus on me, eat, and drink. But nothing helps. She's gone—dissociated or whatever the fuck it's called. When I hold her, she'll give in. Her muscles loosen and she lets her grief flow freely. It seems like a good sign, but everything else is stagnant. She won't even squeeze my hand when I hold it or lean into me like she used to when I wrap her in my arms. She doesn't even try to beg me to take her life.

I manage to get her to drink from a straw, but when I try to feed her something more solid, she doesn't respond. I try to force her mouth open and shove the food inside, but she just sits there, not even chewing. Her lack of response scares the shit out of me, and I curse Dax vehemently when I research feeding tubes and find out there's no way for me to insert one without his medical expertise. I'm not letting him near her for anything in the world.

I consider bringing in a doctor from somewhere else. We have a few clients who are hot-shot surgeons. Having one of them fly in and drive all the way out here would cost a fortune, but that's not what's stopping me. It's the realization that I need to give her what she's been begging for all along.

Death.

It's the only merciful thing to do. And Lavinia deserves it. I can give her what no one has ever given me. A way out. A release. Peace. I want her to have that, and this is the only way.

Even after I've decided, I drag it out for two more days. Two more days of her suffering. I hate myself for it, seeing how she's losing weight, her skin is paling, and she loses the strength to even get her grief out.

On the fifth day, I carry her to the bathroom across the hall, where I sink into the hot water with her. I start by washing her, as if cleaning her could remove her burdens and make her passing easier. But she doesn't need any help where she's going. She won't need *me* where she's going.

I swallow back a knot that's suddenly swelling in my throat.

"I'm sorry," I tell her, holding her close and kissing her skin. "For everything. Bringing you here. Letting all those horrible things happen." I can't even voice any of it. "For not listening to you. But I'll remedy that now. I'll do what I should have done from the start. I'll set you free, my sweet little songbird."

It feels odd as I mentally prepare myself to end her. Weird, twisty sensations stir inside me, and urgent thoughts keep banging to gain entrance to my consciousness. Killing a girl always comes with a rush of power, but I don't feel any of that today.

As much as the change bothers me, it also feels right. Nothing has ever gone as expected with my little songbird, so why should it now? Everything about this scenario is different from my usual kills. I've never killed a girl out of mercy. I've discarded them because they were useless, broken beyond repair, and unsellable, but never because it was what was best for them. I've also never done it in a tub, naked and holding her close. Usually, I'll take them to the incinerator room, feeling the powerful heat of the fire radiating into the space, ready to eat the carcass, as I choke the girl until she passes out, then snap her neck.

I've also never killed someone I care for before. I've never cared for anyone.

The thought sends an achy stab through my chest. Grunting, I ignore it and turn my attention to the task at hand—the delicate creature in my arms.

"You won't feel a thing," I tell my sweet songbird—my beautiful Lavinia—as I tighten my grip to hold her close. "I'll shut off the blood to your brain." I gently slide my hand up her chest, pausing at the edge of her throat. "It will make you pass out." I dip my head close to her ear. "Then, before you come to, I'll snap your neck." I take a deep inhale, branding her scent into my senses. "No pain—no more. I promise."

There's a drip on my hand. A tear, I realize as her chest starts shaking and more tears fall. Leaning closer, I kiss her cheek, tasting her salty tears that are now running in a steady stream.

I start humming, one of the songs she used to sing to me, as I trail my hand up higher. I close it around her slender neck—the one I'll be breaking in a minute. Flexing my fingers, I feel for her arteries, then hold my hand still and slowly press.

A new lump forms at the base of my throat as I feel the strength drain from her body.

"I'm sorry," I tell her, pausing—holding her on the brink for one final moment. "I'm sorry I didn't realize how much you meant to me before it was too late," I say, then press again.

Her hand comes up to grip my arm at her waist. It's a feeble squeeze, but that small gesture damn near breaks me. It's the first movement I've gotten from her since I came back to find her broken, hollowed-out, and voiceless. My hands are suddenly sweaty, and a hazy, nauseous sensation creeps in.

I don't know what's happening to me. Everything curdles inside me as Lavinia's strength fades. My heart pounds as her hand drops down to float in the water, and my airways narrow as she goes limp against me, unconscious.

I've done this so many times that I reflexively readjust my arms, preparing to deliver the needed force to snap her neck.

I place a final kiss on her cheek. This is it.

"Goodbye, my sweet little songbird."

34

LAVINIA

Bright, warm light caresses my face, and something soft and fluffy envelops me. It feels good. Peaceful.

I imagine soaring between the clouds, free and weightless, having shed all the bodily burdens I carried. I always thought everything would black out when I left the world, that the notion of a heaven or an afterlife was just a ruse to make dying more bearable. But that comforting heat on my cheek and the hopeful brightness beyond my closed eyes sure aren't a ruse.

I want to go to it, soak up the warmth and see the light. But my eyes won't quite open yet, and I feel like I'm moving through a haze. It's okay, though, the haze is calm and free of pain, so I take my time.

Slowly, my awareness awakens, and I start sensing other things too. Fresh air and a faint scent of pine. I imagine trees so tall they reach into the clouds, infusing the ethereal space with the calming scent of a forest. I hope I'll get to go into a real forest and see more than treetops. Maybe venture into some mountains and enjoy the peaceful view over undisturbed landscapes.

But something isn't right. As the foggy sensation

lifts, the floaty feeling dissipates. The heat and the light are still there, but so are the bodily and emotional pain I thought I'd shed. Cruel memories flash across my inner eye, breaking up the peaceful clouds and darkening the atmosphere. A heavy and frail sensation tightens around my very bones, and fear and stress creep beneath my skin.

The feeling of being alive.

I know it even before I open my eyes. Once again, faith won't grant me the sweet relief of death. I swallow hard, keeping my eyes closed even as I'm awake enough to open them. I don't want to face the cruel world—the small confinement and the perpetually dim light of my narrow existence. I want to hold on to the scent of pine and the feeling of sunlight for just a moment longer before they slip from my grasp and once again become vague memories.

But reality presses on, urging my attention to my body. The raw sensation in my throat. The lack of sound when I swallow and accidentally whimper. The memory of losing my voice.

My eyes snap open, and a silent scream sticks in my throat as the world draws in and my pulse cranks into a hazardous pace. I try to move, but I'm frozen in place—I've been ever since I lost the only thing left that matters to me. I can't seem to remember how to make my muscles work.

I try to scan the place with my eyes, but they're blurry. All I see is something bright. Sharp. It hurts.

Have I gone blind too?

A hand comes to my shoulder, and I try to scream.

But even as the scream dislodges, all that comes out is a hoarse, wheezy sound, choking me with the horrific confrontation of my lost voice.

"Lavinia, you're safe," a deep, rough, but also soft voice says. A voice that instinctively calms me.

Terror still pulses in my veins as my sight slowly starts working, revealing flashes of a room. A window. I blink, realizing the thing that's blinding me is the sun. A bright round orb of yellow staring at me through an open window.

I shake my head softly, the shock knocking me out of my paralysis. Then a new wave of fear comes rushing as I blink to take in the room. It's simple but beautiful. Tall, arched ceilings, wooden panels, and a fireplace of white stone. But nothing good ever comes of beauty and riches. This is just a new version of hell.

I scream again, the hoarse wheeze reminding me of just how terrible this new hell is. I whip my head from side to side as the scream grows louder in my mind but never escapes into the room.

Two large hands grab my face, and then I'm staring up at the big, brutal man who had become my whole world. The familiar features snap me out of the panic. Then my eyes roam over his face. It feels like a strange dream seeing those features in daylight, surrounded by something that isn't misery and confinement.

There's a low whine at my other side, and I startle as something wet brushes my arm.

"Rex, out," Dorin orders, and I look to see a flash of fur as a big dog runs out of the room.

Returning my attention to Dorin, I just stare at him,

having no idea how to react.

A flood of emotion comes rushing as I realize he came back for me. I part my lips to ask one of the many questions suddenly swirling in my mind. *Why did you come for me? Where are we? Where's Zoltan? Am I safe? Are you keeping me?*

But when I try to give voice to one of them, only air comes out. My world crashes again, the emotions gnawing and biting so hard I close in on myself, shutting down and shutting off. I stare out the window—at treetops rising in the distance, the blue sky, and the bright sun. I don't consider why they're there or how I came to be so close to them. I just stare at them and hold on for dear life, because they're the only thing that will keep me from the spiraling agony of being alive.

35

DORIN

I couldn't do it. I just couldn't. When I had her in the tub and pressed that final kiss to her cheek, I lingered, unable to let go. A small twitch revealed that she was regaining consciousness. I tightened my grip on her, trying to will myself to apply that final burst of force that would snap her neck and grant her the peace she needed.

I thought I was about to do it, but then I was leaning out of the tub instead, ripping the syringe from my jeans pocket, and shoving it into her neck.

Everything from that moment on remains a blur. I can't remember a single thought going through my mind as I lifted her out of the tub, cradling her close to my chest, and carrying her upstairs. I vaguely remember the sensation of staring eyes as I walked naked through the dungeon halls with sleeping beauty nestled in my arms. But I didn't see who was watching. I didn't see anything. Only her. The one person I couldn't bear to lose.

As I lean back on the living room couch and watch the woman in my bed—tucked beneath my sheets, the warm sun caressing her golden locks—a flood of relief swooshes through me. I can't believe how close I came to losing, no, getting rid of her. Twice.

I hate myself for it, with a vehemence that has me grabbing my switchblade and hovering the sharp edge above my skin.

Something I've never told anyone is that my father isn't the only one to take credit for the many scars on my skin. I made some of them myself over the years when the rage and the chaos in my mind were at their worst. The pain of the knife slicing through my skin was the only release I could find. Often, I wanted to do what Lavinia attempted on that first night, but I never did find the strength to turn my wrist and slice right at those arteries.

Maybe that's part of the reason I've been so drawn to her from the start. She possesses the strength I don't have in myself. Being close to her gives me a taste of it, almost like it becomes my own.

Or maybe it's her singing, which is the first non-violent thing to ever quieten the chaos in my mind. Or maybe her angelic appearance that makes me feel close to heaven—something that's always been out of my reach. My father always told me I'd go to hell and would never see the sweet light of heaven. Seeing Lavinia's beautiful light feels like defying him.

But no matter how much I hate myself and want to cut away the pain, I refrain. Because that sweet angel lying in my bed, still as broken and hollow as when I came back and found her broken and voiceless, needs me. I need to be strong. *For her.*

It's been two weeks since I brought her up here. She's doing better than when I took her from her cell and thought I was going to kill her. But better is far from good.

Waking up in my room, seeing the sun, and the open space around her seemed to nudge her out of her empty shell. But she withdrew straight back into it. The change of scenery has done some good, though, beyond that first moment of clarity. I've been able to feed her and make her drink, and she even meets my eyes in short moments. But that's as far as the improvement goes. All day long, she just lies there, staring out the window. She doesn't even nod or shake her head when I ask a question.

Rex gives a slow whine from the bedroom door where he's standing, watching her.

"Sorry, buddy. You can't go in there."

I'm not about to risk scaring her with a huge, curious dog sniffing at her and jumping onto the bed. Rex hates that he can't go to her, but being the good boy he is, he remains just outside the door.

At first, I thought he hovered there because he was weary of the new presence in our quarters, but when I noticed the way he kept whining, I realized he was guarding her. Somehow, even from a distance, he senses that she needs protection. And he's providing that fiercely. He even seems reluctant to leave for our morning runs, and the moment we get back, he rushes to the bedroom door to check on her.

I feel bad for refusing him to go in there. I would rip apart any person trying to keep me from her. But that's the way it has to be.

A knock at the door has Rex going into high alert,

ears pointing into the air as he turns. He remains by the bedroom, though, standing guard, ready to protect my songbird.

"Good boy," I tell him, making a detour to scratch him behind the ear on the way to the door.

I bristle too, preparing to protect, as I open and see Dax standing there—with his girl a step behind him.

Seeing my reaction, Dax lifts his hands. "I come in peace. This is not for me. Emma would really like to see Lavinia."

"Get the hell out of here," I say in a low snarl, hoping Lavinia won't hear. Rex follows my cue, giving a low growl.

Dax sighs. "Mikhail told me she's not doing well."

Fucking Mikhail. He came in here a few days ago to check on the situation. He seemed genuine enough, asking if I needed anything and even accepting the whole Zoltan situation. I don't know why he was so accommodating, but he seemed almost regretful when he watched Lavinia's unmoving body and muttered something about Dax under his breath. His expression was almost wistful when he slapped my shoulder on his way out and said, *I'm happy you've found someone to take care of.*

"I think Emma might be able to help," Dax adds.

"Fuck you." I slam the door in his face. But apparently, I can't get any peace around here. An hour later, there's another knock at the door. This time, it's Mikhail, the meddling motherfucker, *and* Dax's girl.

"What?" I snap. "Don't you have a fucking sale to tend to or something?"

The fucker tries to mosey past me and into my quarters, but I slap a hand to the door frame, blocking his way. "You might own this fucking castle, but *this*"—I gesture to the space behind me—"is *my* place. As long as I do my part around here, you have no right to come in here."

Despite everything with Lavinia, I've been in the dungeon every day, keeping an eye on Mikhail's goddamned incompetent trainers—and paying Zoltan a few visits. He's the perfect outlet for my pent-up rage these days, although it's been hard to keep myself in check enough to not just end him with one quick slash of my knife.

"It's your place, all right," Mikhail agrees. "But I suggest you let me in. Unless you want your girl to wither away in there forever."

Rex parrots me as I make a low growl. "Who the hell are you to come here and—"

I'm about to give him the full brunt of my rage, but Mikhail cuts me off with a sharp command that stuns me into silence. "Quiet!"

As much as I hate this nosy bastard, I respect his authority. He's the only man I could ever answer to. I have no idea how many jobs I've lost because I fucked up my boss in some way or another because I don't do well with authority.

"I'm not here to stick my nose in your business. I'm here to help." He points at the girl behind him, who has retreated three steps down the stairs and is cowering. "She is too. And before you tell me she'll just bother Lavinia and make everything worse, turn on that brain of yours. I know it's in there."

I sneer, but let him continue anyway.

"Remember how Lavinia wanted to take the punishment for Emma? Well, that means she cares about her. So maybe—if you can find it in your thick skull to accept some help—it would do her some good to see her friend. That's why I told Dax about Lavinia's state. *Not* to meddle."

I watch the quiet girl, who's wearing a little black dress that seems to have become her new uniform after Dax decided to make her his. Her hands are obediently gathered behind her back, but I'm not sure they're cuffed, and she's not even wearing the muzzle.

"Cuff her and put the muzzle on her, and I might let her see Lavinia." I won't risk anything.

Mikhail scoffs. The fucker goddamn scoffs. "Do you really think that's the best way to let Emma help her?" Biting his lip, he looks off to the side. "You know, when I first found out about your new little project, I was pissed you wasted your time, not thinking it would last. But as it turned out, you do have a bit of humanity left in you. If you want your girl to get better, you'd damn well better tap into that, or you'll lose her for good when she becomes an irrevocable shell of herself."

I think back to that time when I found Dax's girl by Lavinia's cell. How Lavina begged me not to hurt her. The fierce determination that I mistook for a death wish. This girl means a whole lot to Lavinia for some reason I can't comprehend.

I don't like this—in fact, I hate the idea of someone other than me helping Lavinia. But she's stuck. Seeing her new surroundings and the sun took her a small step out of her paralysis. Maybe this will do the same.

"Okay," I relent. "But I'm staying at her side the whole time."

Mikhail lifts a brow, and I gnash my teeth. There's no way Dax is letting me near his girl. Actually, I can't even believe he offered her help. No less letting her be here without him present—only Mikhail.

I stare at the girl again, noticing the hope lighting up her eyes as she casts a quick glance at me. I wonder if Dax has gone so soft that he's let her convince him to help.

"Fine," I say and take two steps back, giving Mikhail enough space to herd the girl inside without getting within my arm's reach.

"Stay in the living room," Mikhail orders as he steers the girl toward the bedroom. I don't know why the hell I obey. Maybe he's right—I do have a shred of humanity left. Or maybe I'm just selfish and want Lavinia to do better so I can have her back.

It doesn't really matter. I join Rex at the bedroom door as Mikhail brings the girl inside, a small sliver of hope growing in me as she sinks to her knees beside the bed and strokes Lavinia's cheek.

My chest tightens as I watch Lavinia's unmoving frame. My hope is dwindling with each stagnant day, and I feel goddamned helpless. I *hate* it. The chaos in my mind is getting louder by the day. For now, I manage by taking it out on Zoltan. So far, I've pulled off all his nails, cut off all fingers on one hand, shoved various toys up his ass, and pissed on him daily. I considered cutting off his tongue, but right now, I enjoy all his pathetic pleas and hearing him call out for his momma—hearing just how helpless he is. It makes me feel less powerless. But then I come back up here and find Lavinia in the same place I left her, and that toxic feeling slithers back in. All I want to do is lie down behind her and hold her, but I don't dare to touch her. I'm afraid of making her worse. It's probably ridiculous since she sank into me when I held her before I took her up here, but I seem to be as stuck as her.

Dax's girl makes herself comfortable on the floor beside the bed, stroking Lavinia continuously as she speaks in soft tones.

"I'm Emma, by the way," she says after talking about how Dax brought her into the forest the other day and seeing the forest lake. "I'm so happy I get to talk to you now. You have no idea how much it meant to me, hearing your words and your voi—" she stops herself from mentioning Lavinia's voice, her face falling. "I'm so incredibly sorry for what happened to you. I can't even begin to—He shouldn't—" Once again, she stops herself, her features filling with conflicting emotions. "I've lost a lot in this place too, but despite it all, I've somehow found a way to be..." She stares at a tattoo on her lower arm, and a small smile tugs at her lips. "Happy." She returns her attention to Lavinia, splaying her hand over her cheek. "You'll find a way to do the same."

I nearly gasp as Lavinia draws up her shoulders. I can't see her face, but the way Dax's girl leans in and focuses her eyes on Lavinia tells me she's gained eye contact. I almost don't believe it. I'm about to go in there to see for myself, but Mikhail, who's standing close to the door, holds up a hand to stop me.

Anger flares inside me but drowns in a rush of hope as the girl places a hand in Lavinia's open palm and Lavinia actually folds her fingers around it.

"You have Dorin. I don't know him, but"—she casts a tentative glance at me—"I can tell he cares so much about you. He will take care of you. Do you remember when you thought this was a... mental hospital? You said that the methods worked, even though they shouldn't."

Lavinia's head moves with a small nod.

"Maybe it can work again."

Lavinia doesn't seem to respond, and the room goes quiet for a while.

Dax's girl turns her head to look at the window. "The view is really beautiful here. Have you seen it? I mean, up close—not just from the bed."

Lavinia responds with a tiny head shake.

"You should. It's really peaceful. Whenever I feel uncertain and Dax isn't there, I go to the window to watch the mountains and the treetops." She moves up on her haunches and places her open hand on the bed for Lavinia to take. "Can I show you?"

My heart pounds as I wait for Lavinia's reaction. This feels like a crucial moment that will define her future—my future. *Will she stay down or get up?*

Rex stands at full attention, giving a short mewl as if he senses the importance too. I rest my hand on his head, to soothe both him and myself.

My heart skips a beat when Lavinia places her hand in Emma's. I nearly double over as a hefty weight falls off my chest. It's like watching a mirage as Lavinia slowly moves up to sit and the girl at her side drapes a blanket over her shoulders and helps her to her feet.

It takes all my self-control to remain rooted to the spot as Lavinia moves toward the window with slow, staggered steps. I want to go to her, wrap my arm around her waist, and grab her small hand in mine as I lead the way. Make sure she doesn't fall. Protect her. Watching someone else do it is almost painful. Seeing someone else break her out of her numbness is painful.

But then again, I guess I only have myself to blame. I haven't tried much, too scared to do more damage. I've even carried her to and from the bathroom instead of insisting on her walking herself. I'm the one to blame for her almost stumbling on her weak legs as she slowly makes her way to the window.

Rex looks up at me with something that almost feels like a reproach, and I snap out of the self-blame. It's no use. Lavinia can't do shit with it. So I watch instead, taking mental notes of what is working and hoping it will too when I'm the one doing it.

36

LAVINIA

Everything seems to stop as I grab onto the window sill and gaze outside. But it's not in that numb way that shuts my system down. It's more like a swoosh that rips through me, so strong that nothing else works as the energy breathes life into my dead muscles and closed-off brain.

The girl at my side—my friend, Emma—leans in to open the window. A gush of fresh air brings me the scent of pine and damp earth. I've felt it from the bed—seen the sky and the treetops—but it doesn't compare to being this close, tasting it and seeing the whole view. Trees cover the ground below us, sloping with the terrain, and mountains rise in the distance. The sun stands bright and round in the sky, casting its glowing light upon the landscape, and birds chirp a cheery sound. I want to join them—sing an old folk tune to the forest, which my mother taught me, and let my voice soar into the open.

I'll never be able to sing again.

The thought sends a sharp contraction into my muscles, making me gasp, and my throat closes as grief overcomes me. I turn from the window, wanting to go back to the bed and let the numbness swallow me up again. Anything beyond that emptiness hurts too much. The world is already closing in, panic gripping my lungs, claustrophobia squeezing tight as I can't get a word out.

Careful hands grab my arms. "I'm here for you," a soft voice says.

Facing Emma, I lift a finger to my throat and shake my head in utter defeat. *I can't sing.*

"I know," Emma says, voice full of regret. "I know. I'm so, so sorry."

Tears well in my eyes, and my legs start shaking. I dig my fingers into her arms, seeking purchase as the ground is about to fall away beneath me.

Casting my gaze to the side, I meet Dorin's fierce, concerned expression, and that's when everything crumbles. Longing cuts through my insides as I remember how I lost him too—how he left me. My legs cave in as a soundless sob tears through my throat, and I collapse.

Feet pound across the floor, a voice barks warnings, and then the soft hands are gone, replaced by rough, calloused ones that grip me tight and press me into a wide, strong, dangerous chest. But despite the size and roughness, there's no danger. Only honest care.

There's a bustling noise. Feet shuffling, a soft, feminine voice protesting, and a door opening and closing. Leaving, I think. But all I can focus on is the man who won't give me the thing I came to want the most—him—but who holds the power to give me the next best thing.

Please just kill me, please just kill me, I try to say as I grip his T-shirt, but no words come out, only a rough rush of air. I cry harder, the sobs stealing my breath as they claw to come out of my throat in a continuous riptide of empty sound.

The tight grip around me loosens. Hands grab my arms and pull me away from the firm body. The loss makes the panic draw tighter. Waves of dizziness flit through my brain, and nausea rises in my stomach.

"Look at me," a rough voice demands.

I shake my head, and the hands shake me in turn, the voice deepening.

"Look at me, Lavinia."

I snap my eyes open even as I keep shaking my head. I can barely make out the man before me through the blinding haze. I only see the outlines of rough features, a bald head, and the line of a scar.

"Breathe," he says with such a steady force that it makes the haze retreat for a short moment. His insistent eyes become clear, and so do his lips as he rounds them and draws a sharp breath.

Automatically, I follow, heaving so much air into my starved lungs that it's painful. But I can't hold on to it. The air crashes back out immediately and sends me back into hyperventilation.

The strong hands move me around, placing me against the bed. Big palms cup my cheeks as a large figure crowds me. But as Dorin's voice filters through the haze again, the imposing figure doesn't feel threatening.

"Breathe, Lavinia." Tightening his hold on my face, he leans in and presses his lips to mine. With a long exhale, he breathes air into me. It doesn't bring me the oxygen I need, but it prompts me to draw a slow, deep breath of my own when he disconnects our lips.

"Again," he says, his lips hovering right before mine, the rush of air caressing them and sparking a desire to feel—something, anything. *Him.*

I manage to draw several steady breaths. The haze dissipates, my vision clears, and Dorin appears before me. The sight nearly sends me straight back into a fit of panic, knowing it's just temporary. I've only regained him to lose him again.

But the words he speaks send the panic cowering.

"I'll never—not ever—let you go again." He says it with such ferocity I can't doubt him. "You're the only person who has ever mattered to me, and I can't bear to lose you." Digging his fingers into my cheeks, he draws a shuddery breath and rests his forehead against mine. "I'm so, so sorry I tried to sell you. Please believe me. Please forgive me. I had no idea what I was doing. I still don't. But I know one thing. I *need* you." Pulling back, he watches me with a startling plea in his eyes. "Please don't ask me to kill you. I can't bear to live without you."

The grief draws back as I stare at him, shocked at his honest confession. I don't know what I'd say even if I could speak. I have no idea how to live without my voice, but leaving Dorin doesn't seem like an option either. As much as he has hurt me, I'm still eternally grateful for him and the things he's done for me—the spark he awoke in me, no matter how briefly it shone. I don't know if I'll ever be able to get that will to live back, but for now, I need him to know one thing.

I forgive him.

Trying to convey my sincerity through my eyes, I lift my hand and press it to his chest. I make a slow nod, mouthing the words, *I forgive you.*

A lost look descends over his features, and his eyes become shiny with tears as he watches my lips like he can't believe it.

Mirroring his grip on me, I reach up to cup his cheeks as I look him deep in the eyes and mouth the words again. *I forgive you.*

It's like the weight of the world drops from his shoulders as he falls forward, burying his head into my neck. He pulls my body against his, supporting us in an awkward position with a hand gripping the bed. His breaths come in shuddery gusts against my neck as he holds me so close I can barely breathe. I band my arms around him, holding on for dear life. And I guess it does. He's the only thing keeping me here, making me not beg him for death. Making me want to stay.

Slowly, his ragged breaths calm, his furious grip on me loosens, and he scoots into a more comfortable position, sitting beside me, head still hidden in the crook of my neck.

It's not until a clipped bark sounds from across the room that he lifts his head. Uncertainty flickers across his face as he glances behind him to the dog at the door, then to me.

His voice is tentative as he speaks. "I'd like to introduce you to someone. If that's okay with you?"

I glance back at the dog. I've felt its presence—heard its sounds—continuously while being here, but have been too numb to see or truly notice the dog. It's big and alert but looks friendly enough. And I trust Dorin to protect me. So I nod.

"Rex, come here," Dorin calls, and paws scrape against the floor as the big German Shepherd rushes into the room and rounds the bed. "Sit," Dorin orders, just before the dog reaches me. It drops onto its butt even as it sticks it snout out, sniffing toward me.

"Lavinia, this is Rex. He's been living with me since he was a small pup, too young to leave his mother." A hint of sadness crosses his features as he reaches out to stroke the dog's thick fur. "I found him in an abandoned house. He was lost and alone, so I took him in." His eyes roam my face meaningfully as if he realizes that he found me the same way. Alone and lost. He took me in. I feel the resemblance too, and a sense of connection makes me reach for the dog.

"Let him smell your hand first." Dorin takes my hand and guides it up to Rex's nose, and he sniffs away eagerly. I jerk when Rex gives my fingers a big lick, but it's more out of surprise than fear. "Easy now, buddy," Dorin says. "We don't want to scare her." Turning to me, he says, "Rex is very protective of you. He's sensed that you needed it. He's been standing at the bedroom door every waking hour and sleeping there to watch over you."

I look from Dorin to the big dog, almost unable to believe it. I haven't done anything to earn their protection, yet somehow, I've called upon the protectiveness in both of these two mighty, dangerous creatures. Leaning into Dorin, I reach out to touch Rex's fur. He reacts by sticking his tongue out of his mouth, and his tail sweeps eagerly across the floor as I start stroking.

"Is it okay if he comes closer?" Dorin asks.

I nod.

"Free," Dorin tells Rex, and he jumps to his feet and scuttles closer, sniffing at my arms and all but climbing into my lap to smell my hair. I draw back a bit but continue stroking, nonetheless, enjoying his eager exploration and the feeling of his soft fur brushing my skin. I want to burrow my head into it and give the dog a big hug. When he keeps sniffing, poking his snout at me and swishing his tail happily, I end up doing it.

I wrap my arms around his neck and bury my head in his fur, feeling a rush of... life—desire to go on—as I soak up the happy, exuberant energy of the big dog. He proves to be surprisingly cuddly, angling his head to the side, almost like a cat, when I scratch behind his ear. He crowds me in return, pressing his head into me in a hug of its own.

When I glance at Dorin, he's watching us with a stunned expression, full of awe. A big smile lights up his eyes and makes his lips widen as he holds my gaze, and that's when I realize I'm smiling.

Hope blooms in my chest. It's a careful kernel, but it's there, and for once, it doesn't just feel like a small glimmer in the darkness, but a full bright ray of sunshine that might shine upon me. I don't dare to believe it might be real, but the feeling remains as Dorin lifts me onto the bed and lies down behind me, stroking me gently while Rex lies before me and I fall asleep with my hands nestled in his fur.

37

DORIN

A few days later, I suck up my pride and ask Mikhail to bring Dax's girl back. Lavinia has been doing better, sitting up in bed, letting me take her to the window, and letting me read to her while Rex curls up at her side. But as much as I want to fix her myself, I want to do what's best for her even more, and letting her see her friend might speed things along.

An annoying-as-hell smile spreads over Mikhail's face. "I told—"

"Don't even start," I cut him off before he can put more words to his ridiculous self-satisfaction. "Are you gonna bring her to Lavinia or not?"

His expression sobers as he sighs. "I'll try. But I'm not sure Dax will let me after the way you broke our deal the last time."

My voice becomes a frustrated growl as I fail to rein in my anger. "I didn't hurt her. I didn't even fucking touch her."

"No, but you broke our deal."

"Whatever. If he wants to come, he can. But he's staying in the living room, and you're staying with the girls." I can't believe I'm suggesting this—that I'm actually allowing Dax into my quarters after what he did. What annoys me even more is that I'm starting to understand why he'd allow his girl to go to my place without him. *Shit,* I'm becoming soft like him. Gnashing my teeth together, I ignore the realization.

"I'll ask him," Mikhail agrees, and before he can throw more smug comments my way, I trudge on.

When he calls me in the evening to let me know Dax has agreed and they'll drop by in the morning, I realize it might be a really fucking bad idea to bring Dax here. The mere sight of him might traumatize Lavinia. I'm about to shut the whole thing down but decide to ask her first.

The sight that meets me in the bedroom loosens some of the knots in my chest. Lavinia and Rex are lying on the bed, him resting his head on his paws, looking very contented, while she gently rubs his fur. With her back turned to me, I can't see her face, but those small movements of her fingers and her relaxed position are enough to drain some of the tension from my body.

I carefully scoot onto the bed, leaning against the headboard beside her and running my hand over her soft locks. She gives a restful sigh, and relief washes away a little more of the tension stuck in my shoulders.

I close my eyes for a beat, just soaking up the moment. I can't believe we're actually here, all three of us. I've fantasized about this but never dared to believe I could have something as calm and comfortable in my life. But here I am.

Lavinia's breathing is deepening, verging on sleep, when I realize a lot longer than a moment has passed.

"Lavinia. My sweet so—" I stop myself before saying songbird. "My sweet girl. I have something to ask you before you fall asleep."

She slowly turns to look at me, eyes blinking drowsily.

I stroke the hair from her face and brush my knuckles over her cheek. "I want to bring your friend—Emma—here again. But since I fucked up the last time, Dax won't let her come alone. He'll stay in the living room with me, and Mikhail will be in here with the two of you. You'll be safe. I'll protect you. Would that be okay with you?"

A wealth of emotion flashes through her eyes, and I think the mere idea is going to throw her into a fit of panic. But then the storm settles. Acceptance calms her expression, and she nods.

"Are you sure?"

She reaches up to take my hand and nods again.

I watch her closely for a moment. "Okay," I agree when I don't see any further signs of the conflicting emotions. "They'll be here in the morning."

* * *

Dax and I take a seat at each end of the couch, gluing our eyes to the bedroom, not casting a single glance at one another. I'm fucking jealous of Rex, who scurries into the bedroom along with Mikhail and the girls. He won't leave Lavinia's side for a single moment. When I took them for a walk in the forest yesterday, he remained right next to her instead of bouncing off to explore like he usually does. I want to do the same. I hate it every time I have to leave to tend to my responsibilities in the dungeon, but knowing Rex watches over her makes it easier.

The girls take a seat on the bed, their backs to us to watch the view outside. I want to bark at Mikhail when he sits in my recliner and fucking takes his phone out. He's supposed to keep an eye on them. But then again, I don't think Dax could convince his girl to hurt Lavinia, just like I couldn't convince Lavinia to hurt his girl. And Rex is as good a guard as any. He might look all cute and cuddly as he rests his head on Lavinia's lap, enjoying her petting, but he'd tear anyone apart who tried to harm her.

I stay aware of Dax the whole time without looking at him. He seems to do the same, his posture rigid, tension rolling off him in waves. I don't know how long we sit like that, both on high alert, not saying anything but being fully aware of each other. Maybe a whole hour.

Mikhail snaps us both out of the stiff tension with a sudden clap of his hands. "Chop, chop, time to leave."

Pressing my hands to my thighs, I prepare to burst into action, but Mikhail is laid-back as ever as he pockets his phone and gets up.

Casting a glance at Dax, I quickly remove my hands from my thighs as I find him in the same position. He gives me a cold look when his girl comes out, and he's quick to guide her toward the door, away from me.

I scoff quietly. He can protect her all he wants, but eventually, I'll get to her.

She leans up to whisper something to him, making him pause.

"Do *not* go to him," he stresses in a low voice, then grabs her arm as she turns to me.

Her eyes flit up and down, between me and the floor, and her chin lowers in deference. Maybe fear. Part of me wants to scoff and ridicule her, but then there's a part that has me tilting my head slightly, making my eyes glide up and down her delicate frame, taking in her submissive stance. She looks like a nervous little kitten, and I almost want to go scratch her behind the ear.

Shoving the ridiculous thought aside, I demand, "What is it?"

She licks her lips, then says in a voice so soft I almost don't hear, "You should get her a violin."

Before I can inquire to see if I heard right, she's out the door, scurrying away—and there's that kitten image again. I almost understand why Dax is so damn smitten with her. *Almost.* But it's still ridiculous how soft he's become for a woman, letting her affect him like that.

I make my way to the bedroom and lift Lavinia onto my lap, needing to feel her close—to know she's safe. Rex jumps on the bed and nudges his head between us, and I readjust Lavinia to make room for him.

That's when I once again realize I've gone soft myself. And not just for Rex, but for a fucking girl too. *I'm just like Dax.*

The thought bugs the hell out of me, and I try to deny it. But as Dax comes here with his girl several times over the next few days, the similarities become glaring. What I also realize is that it might not be such a bad thing. As much as I found Dax weak for caring for a girl, I now find a certain respect for his fierce protectiveness toward her. She might be his weakness, but she's also his strength—someone giving him the will to go through fire. Just like I'd do for Lavinia. As much as I feel weak and scared of losing her, she makes me feel strong too. When I'm around her, the voices in my head fade, dulling my temper and strengthening my control, and seeing the way she responds to me—the way I'm once again healing her—makes me feel powerful.

When Dax leaves that day, I give him a curt nod. His brows draw tight, suspicion darkening his eyes. The idiot doesn't understand that I'm trying to convey my appreciation. I sure am not about to put words to it, though.

But the nod was genuine. Lavinia lights up whenever Dax's girl is here. Her writing on the notepad I've given her becomes more eager with each time her friend is here. It even rubs off on the amount she communicates with me. It's still mostly practicalities, but every now and then, she'll write something that Rex did while I was gone, like when he chased a fly and almost choked on it when he caught it. Seeing her eyes light up when she wrote that nearly had me jumping her like a feral beast in heat, but I'm still holding back with her, sticking to kisses and caresses, not wanting to push too hard, too fast.

So even though I'm not prepared to voice my gratitude, I just might end up sparing both Dax and his girl.

I'm not happy about forfeiting my vengeance, letting Dax get away with taking her fucking voice. But as I take Emma's advice and order a violin for Lavinia, a new hope grows inside me—that Lavinia might gain a new voice.

38

LAVINIA

"I have something for you," Dorin says one morning when he comes into the bedroom.

I've just gotten dressed, ready to go for what has become our regular morning walk. Rex hovers around me as I walk to the bed to sit. My legs are still weak after such a long period of inactivity, and Rex seems to sense it, always at my side from the moment I leave the bed, ready to offer support if needed.

Dorin comes to sit beside me, a long cardboard box in his arms. Setting it on his lap, he says, "Open it."

Rex jumps onto the bed, rushing around us and sticking his snout between us to sniff the contents suspiciously.

"I swear he was a guard dog in his former life," Dorin says, giving Rex a good head scratch. "And a lap dog in the life before it."

Leaning down to Rex with a smile, I part my lips to tell him what a good boy he is. A pang of longing contracts my chest as I snap my lips shut, remembering I can't give voice to those words, and have to settle for showing him with a kiss on his head.

"He knows," Dorin says, voice full of sympathy and understanding.

I lift my eyes to his, pausing in my movements at his knowing gaze.

"Your touch and your body language are plenty to tell him how much you appreciate him."

Vulnerability flushes over me. And gratitude. I don't know how, but Dorin has come to read me with scary precision. I often don't even have to use the notepad when I need something, and often, Dorin predicts my needs before I even know them myself. Even though I try to hide the constant grief, he can tell when it's about to get the better of me, taking me in his arms and whispering soothing words until I let go and let the hurt flow freely in the safe embrace of his arms.

"Open," Dorin repeats, nodding to the box.

Lifting my hands, I carefully open the top and lean in to see what's inside. My breath stops when I see a black case hidden beneath layers of paper. *It can't be.* Pulling the wrapping aside, I see the shape of the case. Wide and rounded at one end, long and narrow at the other. My hand flies to my mouth, and I shake my head as I lift my eyes to Dorin.

It can't be. Pinch me.

"A violin," he confirms, and tears spring to my eyes at the confirmation.

I reach my hands into the box but pull them back out, feeling like there's a catch. A price to pay.

Reading my reaction, he says, "It's for you. You may use it whenever and however much you like. It doesn't come at a cost. I'm not Zoltan." His eyes darken. "I'm never gonna put a price on your happiness."

His words have me reaching for the notepad as a surge of fear rises within me. I had all but forgotten about Zoltan trying to buy me, too ridden with grief—too numb—to do anything other than take one day at a time.

Where is he? I scribble and hold the paper up briefly. *Will he come for me here? Am I safe here?*

I know Dorin must have somehow overturned the sale, and I trust that he'll do everything in his power to keep me safe, but I also know the kind of resources and reach Zoltan has.

Darkness sweeps across Dorin's features. "That man is *never* going to touch you again."

How? I write, the huge letters filling half the page. I show them to Dorin, then rip the page off to start on a fresh one. *You don't know him. He'll come for me. He has—*

Dorin grabs my hand, stopping me mid-sentence.

"I *know*," he says fiercely. "He's here. In a cell. Begging for his momma."

I give a confused shake of my head.

"Don't you remember the promise I made? That I'll kill him?"

Biting my lips together, I nod slowly.

"That promise still stands. But I'm taking my time. I want him to suffer for what he did to you."

The snarl forming on his lips as he says the word *suffer* almost makes me draw back. But I know Dorin. So I lean forward instead, grabbing on to his T-shirt as my heart pounds with a speed that makes the world whir around me. I sit there for several minutes, feeling the steady thuds of his heart and letting it be the beat that grounds me.

When my own heart settles in a regular rhythm, I lean back to write again. *What have you done to him?*

"Are you sure you want to know?" he asks, brows furrowing in a grave expression.

I need to know, I write. I look toward the window for a moment, then continue. *I want to see.*

Dorin sighs. "It's not a pretty sight. I've cut off most of his fingers, taken one of his eyes, and he's coming down with a severe infection in one of his legs."

I underline the last four words I wrote and hold the notepad up, tapping against them to convey how much I need this. Zoltan has been a constant fear gnawing at the back of my mind, biting deep into my bones, ever since I fled from him. I need to know that I no longer have to fear him.

"Okay," he relents with a sigh. "I'll take you to see him. But first, I want you to open your present."

Gently, I reach down and take the violin case in my hands. A surge of something powerful rushes through me as I bring it into my lap and pop the clasps open. Closing my eyes, I lift the lid, still unable to believe I'll find a real violin in there.

Time slows as I open my eyes and see a beautiful, shiny violin. I just stare at it. The polished wood, the taut strings, and the elegant curve of the body. I haven't touched a violin for years. I don't even know if I remember how to play anymore.

Dorin seems to be holding his breath when I glance up at him.

"Play for me," he says, his breathy voice full of hope.

Carefully, I wrap my fingers around the neck and lift the instrument out of its case. A shuddery breath escapes me as I rest it on my shoulder. Plucking two strings at a time, I listen to the soft vibrations as I tune them. Then I pick up the bow, and time comes to a standstill as I hover it right above the strings.

The room is completely silent, full of anticipation. All three of us—Dorin, Rex, and me—seem to hold our breaths. I search my mind for a melody. Something I used to play. It takes a full minute, but finally, one pops up.

Closing my eyes, I press my finger to a string and draw the bow across it. The pure sound makes me shudder with a stuttered breath. I pause, lift the bow again, and sweep it across the string. This time, I hold the movement, guiding the bow while sliding my finger to the next note.

Before I know it, I'm playing one of my favorite tunes. Memories come rushing. My mother singing along, my sister dancing, her golden hair billowing as she swirls, her soft laughter echoing through our cozy living room. I play for them. For the good memories and for the love I still hold for them. When I draw the last note and fade it into silence, I expect the same sharp pain that usually accompanies the memory of them to slash through me. But it doesn't come. The grief is there, but it's more like a quiet wistfulness floating among all the good memories and the knowledge that they're at peace.

When I open my eyes, a flood of different memories come rushing as I see the man before me. Dorin lifting me out of the tub, Dorin holding me when all the emotions come flooding out, and Dorin erasing the cruel memories in my body by claiming me himself. All the bad memories are there too, but just like the grief, they mix with the good ones, no longer dominating my mind or tearing all the good ones apart.

Hope blooms inside me. I smile. At Dorin and at Rex. Then I lift the bow again and play.

* * *

"Are you ready?" Dorin asks with a grave expression when he comes back from the dungeon in the evening.

Shutting the book I was reading, I scoot away from Rex to sit on the edge of the bed and nod.

Dorin is quiet as he waits for me to put on a bit more clothes and shoes, then leads the way down the many stairs, through a couple of corridors, and down more stairs leading to a heavy iron door. He glances at me one final time before pressing his hand to the biometric scanner.

This is it. My heart thuds against my rib cage as I prepare to return to the place that built me up and broke me down, only to have me go through the same process all over again.

Dorin takes my hand in a firm hold as we enter the dungeon. I can't believe I've spent several months down here, without the sun, surrounded by these barren halls. It's even harder to believe I found some kind of peace here. The walls seem to whisper stories of violence and misery, and the dry scent of the basement is like a virus in my throat, scratching and refusing to let me forget where we are even when I close my eyes. But as much as the place unnerves me, it also awakens a strange sort of buzzing within me.

Glancing at Dorin, I think of all the things he did to me down here—the electro "therapy," the straitjacket, even the punishment. A hum stirs deep in my belly. A desire to feel his darkness unleashed upon me again. I'm not ready yet, but at that moment, I know I'm going to ask him to bring me down here at some point.

Dorin stops at a green metal door and turns to me. "It's not a pretty sight."

Nothing he can say will change my mind. I need to see Zoltan. It's the only way to stop the nightmares and the clawing fear choking me in fits of flashbacks. So I nod again.

The biometric scanner beeps, and Dorin opens the door.

A foul smell assaults my senses, making me cover my nose and mouth. Blood, urine, rot, and misery. Closing my eyes, I steel myself before following Dorin into a small windowless cell with four barren walls, a toilet and a sink, and a thin mattress in the corner. I gasp at the sight of the man lying on it. At first, I think it's not him—Dorin has the wrong man. There's none of the arrogant confidence or ruthless pride I know from Zoltan, and the frail body with protruding ribs is nothing like the well-defined abs of Zoltan's body.

But then I step closer, and the decrepit man lifts his eyes—or rather, eye. And there's that cruel, soulless look that not even his charming smiles could cover up. Despite the swollen, dark tissues around his bloodshot eye and the other socket being empty, it's clear. It is him.

His gaze fills with scorn as he watches me. Coughing, he clears his voice and licks his cracked lips. "The bitch is back," he says in a voice so weak I want to laugh.

I rake my eyes down his body. Cuts and bruises cover every inch of it, and multiple fingers and toes are missing.

"Do you want me to cut out his tongue?" Dorin asks.

I stare at the decrepit man before me, and this time, I actually smile as fear wipes out the scorn in his eyes and he tries to scoot back on the mattress. An agonized groan escapes him at the movement, and his hand comes down to cover his thigh protectively. Not even the bandage there can cover up the state of his leg. Deep shades of red and blue, swollen tissue, and even peeling skin. This man is dying—unless someone cuts off his leg.

An unfamiliar surge rushes through me as I watch him. He tries to cast me another hateful look but fails miserably as he pants and winces. It's power I'm feeling, I realize. Seeing this man who has always made me feel worthless and weak in this state makes me feel powerful.

My pulse beats with purpose as I turn to Dorin and point at Zoltan's leg while making a kicking motion.

He immediately understands my silent question. "You may do whatever you want. Except for killing him. I don't want you to carry that around."

Not wasting a second, I go to Zoltan with determined steps. Staring him deep in the eye, I lift my foot above his injured leg, relishing the terror widening his gaze, and slam my foot down. I prepare for some kind of retaliation, quickly stepping back, but all I get is an agonized wail as Zoltan curls up weakly. It makes me smile, and I step closer again and kick his arms away from his leg before slamming my foot back down on the wound.

Adrenaline becomes a heady swoosh through my veins as I keep kicking and stomping. Hate gathers within me, but instead of coiling and constricting, it rushes out with each burst of violence. The world draws back, giving me tunnel vision. I put in more force, kicking with all my might—all over. His leg, his stomach, and even his face. Blood smears my shoe, but the sight only drives me on. Because for once, it's not my blood.

A voice speaks somewhere in the background, but I don't hear it. All my ears notice are Zoltan's pathetic whimpers as he begs me to stop and calls out for his mother. *Pathetic little prick.* I deliver another kick to his gut, enjoying the way it makes him gag. I lift my foot again, but someone grabs me from behind and pulls me back.

"Enough," a deep voice demands, but it's not enough to stop the rage rushing through me. If anything, it intensifies it. I go frantic. Hanging in the air, a thick arm banded around my chest, I kick and hit blindly, writhing and jerking. Raw wheezing sounds escape my throat in lieu of screams. I keep going, struggling with all my might, scratching at Dorin's skin. But I'm not going anywhere. He has me trapped against his chest, holding me like I'm nothing but a flapping bird. But instead of feeling weak in his arms, I realize there's safety in his strength. Because he doesn't use it to hurt me. Dorin is strong enough to take the storm of my rage and get us both safely through it.

When I finally go still, he turns me around and lowers himself to his haunches, gathering me between his legs.

"I've got you," he whispers, peppering tiny kisses over my head. "You're safe. He can't ever hurt you again."

I don't know how long I sit there. At some point, I start shaking, the pained groans behind me go quiet, and then the shaking fades again.

Finally, I lift my head to look at Dorin.

Brushing his fingers over my forehead, he moves my hair from my sweaty face.

"Do you want me to end him now or let him suffer more? I might be able to keep him alive a while longer with antibiotics."

I stare into the distance as I consider. The hateful part of me that has my blood pulsing, craving eternal vengeance, wants to prolong the suffering. But there's nothing peaceful in revenge, and what I crave more than anything else is peace.

Leaning my head on his shoulder, I consider for a moment. I'm exhausted. Spent. Done.

I'm done.

Certainty is firm in my hand as I face Dorin and make a slicing motion across my throat.

Dorin gets up, holding a hand against my back as I move into a more stable position, then closes the distance to the mattress with four long strides. Zoltan seems to wake from whatever unconscious state he was in as

Dorin grabs his head, and a raw wail bounces off the barren walls just before Dorin twists his head around in a rapid movement that gives a loud crack, then leaves the room in silence. The echo dies out, and I stare at Zoltan's limp body, shock and horror warring to get the upper hand. But as my eyes flit away from the man who was my worst nightmare, to the one who is my savior, another feeling wins out. *Relief. All-consuming, overwhelming relief.*

I draw a long, freeing sigh and smile at Dorin. It's a careful smile, but it's there. *Thank you,* I mouth. Finally, I'm free. For the first time since I lost everything, I can see real hope ahead of me.

39

DORIN

“Do you still want me to kill you?” I ask Lavinia in the evening after I’ve bathed her, held her, and fed her. I’m not sure this is the right time to ask, but I need to know.

I’ve given this a lot of thought and have decided. If she wants me to take her out, I’ll do it. But I won’t break her neck like I usually do. I won’t let her go alone. With her, I’ve found a strength that will allow me to do what I’ve wanted to do so many times throughout my life—what I no longer want as long as I have her. I’ll get us enough tranquilizer to kill a horse. I’ll put it in the sweetest wine I can get, pour each of us a glass, drink it together, then take her to bed and hold her. She’ll pass away in my arms, and I’ll slip away from this world along with her.

But as much as I’ve come to terms with this idea, accepting that I’ll grant her a way out if that’s what she wants, I dearly hope she’ll choose another way. To stay with me.

Time stops as she stares off into the distance. Everything inside me teeters, getting ready to break. When she turns her head to me, my heart is lodged in my throat along with a thick lump of grief. But then she shakes her head.

I just watch her for a moment, stunned. Unable to believe what I'm seeing.

At my shocked silence, she grabs both my hands and looks deep into my eyes as she makes several unmistakable shakes of her head. Then she presses her hand against my heart, and I damn near break into tears.

She wants to stay. With me.

"Are you sure?" I say, still not able to believe. "I'll set you free if that's what you want. I'll do it for you."

She presses her hand harder to my chest as her lips move. *You,* she mouths. *I want you.*

Relief bursts through me with a force that sends my whole damn system reeling. But in the wake of the relief comes a thought I haven't even considered. I've been so sure she'd choose death that I couldn't imagine any other outcome.

My heart pounds as I say, "I can't release you into the world. If you stay, you stay with me. I'm not ever letting you go. I can't do it." The idea of someone else claiming her has a surge of rage burning through my veins, making me open and close my fists with barely restrained violence.

Her face remains calm. Accepting. Her hand stays in place over my pounding heart.

"I'm not a good man. I don't deserve you. I'm selfish and I'm cruel. I won't be cruel to you, but I can't change who I am. I can't leave this place. This is where I belong."

She holds her hand up, making a writing motion.

I reach out for the notepad and pen on the bedside

table and hand it to her.

Holding my breath, I wait as she writes. It only takes two seconds before she holds the pad up to me and I read the words.

Me too.

I just stare at her as she turns the paper to write more words. This time, it takes a little longer as she scribbles down several lines.

I press my hand to hers when she turns the paper and once again holds her hand to my chest.

Ever since I lost my family and my home, I've been lost. I've been to so many places. Grand mansions, dingy bars. Every place was just a new hell. But then you found me. This place has been hell too, but most of all, it has set me free. You have set me free. I don't want to search anymore. I want to stay here with you.

Grabbing the notepad, I fling it aside, grab her head between my hands, and crush my lips to hers. "You're mine," I breathe between kisses. "The most beautiful creature I've ever laid my eyes on."

Her hands wrap around my neck, holding on as she succumbs to my possessive kisses.

"I'm going to brand you, so you'll never forget. So everyone can see who you belong to."

She arches into me at those words.

"I'll put a collar on you with my name. I'll chain you up, so you won't escape—even though I know you won't try. I'll do it just because I can."

A long breath—a soundless moan—escapes her, and her fingers dig into my skin as she leans deeper into my kiss.

"You want that?" I grip the back of her neck hard, leaning away to watch her reaction.

Her eyes are wide and glazed with desire as she nods.

"You want me to brand my name into your skin?"

She nods again.

"Give you new marks to erase the old ones—to stake my claim?"

Her nod grows more eager, and I can't help myself. I pull my switchblade from my pocket and pop it open.

"You want to bleed for me?"

Her eyes become pleading as I hold the knife to a scar on her chest. But it's not a plea for me to stop. It's an urgent plea for me to stake my claim.

So I do just that.

I press the knife into her skin and drag it across the scar. I growl as blood pebbles around the blade, smearing her milky white skin in crimson. The sight has my cock growing painfully hard, straining against my pants.

"Take out my cock," I demand, and she fumbles eagerly with the button and the zipper to get it out. "It's about time I claim your pussy," I rasp as she takes my length into her hands and licks her lips.

Slipping her other hand down her stomach, between her legs, she pushes her panties aside and watches me expectantly. Her eyes flicker down to the knife and to my cock, and her hips strain upward, begging for more.

I give it to her. Both the knife and my cock. As I position my hips above hers, letting her guide my hard length to her opening, I press the knife to a new scar. Her eyes roll back as I cut her, her lips parting to let out a hard, pleasured breath.

"Fuck, you're perfect," I say, cutting again, sinking into her soaking wet pussy. "Shit, you're wet." It's been years since I took a girl in this hole, and I groan at the slick sensation—the warm, wet heat engulfing me. Her walls clench tight, inviting me in.

"You're mine," I growl. "Mine to hurt, mine to own, mine to protect."

I fling my knife aside and grab her waist. Squeezing her fragile body, I slam into her, demanding her eyes stay on me with the sheer force of my furious expression. "Mine," I growl as I pound into her with punishing thrusts.

Her brow draws tight in a pained expression even as her breaths come in heavy, pleasured pants, her hips bucking into me, seeking more. Seeing the combination of her pleasure and pain damn near drives me insane.

"Touch yourself," I demand, wanting—needing—to take her with me over the edge. I don't know if I can hold that long, but I damn well intend to try.

My balls draw up tight, and the way her mouth moves in cute little ohs and ahs as she slips a finger over her clit nearly pushes me over. Her breathing immediately speeds up, and I smile as I sense her closing in so quickly.

"That's it. Come for me. Show me who you belong to."

You, she mouths, and seeing that word on her lips becomes my undoing. I growl—a sound more beast than man—as I spurt my cum inside her. She follows right along, coming apart beneath me with shuddery jerks and gasps, her free hand clawing at my skin as her eyes roll back.

I stay on top of her for a moment as she comes down, enjoying the sight of her, sated and satisfied. Then I roll onto my side and gather her in my arms. I hold her there for a long while, enjoying the peace that envelops us—the quietness that descends over my mind.

"Thank you," I say, kissing her temple. "My sweet, pretty Lavinia. My beautiful little songbird."

Her entire body goes rigid at that last word. I haven't said it since she lost her voice, but I've thought it so many times.

Pressing a hand to her cheek, I turn her head to meet her pained expression. "You are," I insist. "You're still my songbird."

She shakes her head ardently, squeezing her eyes shut as a world of pain descends over her features.

With a resolute motion, I get off the bed, go to the living room, and grab the violin.

"Sit up," I demand when I come back.

Hurt is lodged deep inside her blue eyes when she opens them and reluctantly moves to sit on the edge of the bed.

"Play," I order.

Her brows are tightly knitted, her jaw clenched hard as she takes the violin and places it on her shoulder. But she plays anyway. At first, it's stiff and soulless, but as her fingers dance over the strings and her hand sweeps the bow back and forth, her shoulders drop, the furrow in her forehead smooths out, and her jaw loosens. Her eyes fall shut as she becomes one with the music, and the music takes on a whole new life and vigor.

I carefully move to sit on the bed beside her, closing my eyes as I let her music wash over me. Rex pads over too, resting his head on my thigh as she plays.

Images of the mountains, the lake between the trees, and the magnificent view from the cliff appear before my inner eye. Sunshine shimmering on the water, a gentle breeze blowing through the trees. Pretty blue eyes watching me with trust and vulnerability. So much strength.

The music stops, and I open my eyes to meet the gaze of my dreams.

"See. You're still my songbird." I grab her chin before she can shake her head. "You still sing as beautifully as ever. Just with a different instrument."

The defeat in her eyes remains despite my words, so I continue.

"It was the emotions you poured into your music that silenced my mind. It still is. It doesn't matter if you sing or play the violin. The effect is the same."

As I speak, the sorrow draws back, replaced by that open vulnerability she's shown me so many times.

"You're still my songbird."

This time, she doesn't protest. Tears pool in her bright eyes as she stares at me, hope mixing into the sorrow. Hope I put there. Hope that isn't just healing her, but healing me as well.

She grabs my hand and squeezes it for a long moment. A *thank you.* Then she places the violin back on her shoulder and lifts the bow, accepting my name for her.

She's still my songbird. Always will be.

Dear reader

Thank you so much for reading! I hope you enjoyed the book! If you did, please leave a review. Just a few lines make a big difference and mean the world to an indie author like me.

To get direct updates, special giveaways, MMC takeovers, and exclusive sneak peeks, sign up for my newsletter at www.ellajacobs.com.

Lots of dark love

Ella

ALSO BY ELLA JACOBS
Excerpt from In His Cage

Money is power; power is danger.
Stay away from rich men.

Aleksandr Pletnev was supposed to be the man who made my dreams come true. Instead, he kidnaps me and locks me in a cage of gold.

Now I exist under his brutal command, trapped and at his mercy.

My captor will do just about anything to assert his ownership and break me into acceptance. But it's not the whippings or degradations that break me. It's when his darkness gives way to tender gentleness.

I fight with everything I have, but he keeps insisting that I need the stability of his command, and soon I don't know if I'm losing or finding myself.

* * *

"Keep walking," a deep voice commands, all too calmly.

I want to turn my head—see who's got the nerve to grab me and press a knife to my back in broad daylight. But I can't. Fear has me paralyzed, unable to think or act. My legs are the only thing working, and only because they have to.

All I can see from the corner of my eye is his left side—white and black clothes, tall and broad frame. He's so tall his face is hidden way above my head where I don't dare cast my eyes up. His fingers are large enough to encompass my upper arm in an unbreakable grip. It's not forceful, but the potential strength is palpable. He could easily snap my bones.

Icy shivers skate down my skin, and my legs quiver, threatening to give in. But fear is not the only thing churning in my stomach. There's this feeling of powerlessness that tugs at something deep inside me—some magnetic pull, against all rationality, that flutters and sends heat coursing through my veins.

It's his presence. It looms over me like a great building casting its shadow over several blocks, calm and powerful. Commanding in a most masculine way that speaks to my feminine soul and keeps my heart from speeding too fast. It's like the unwavering stability steadies me through the fear that wreaks havoc on my insides.

Fuck. I must be sick. There's nothing alluring about a stranger who presses a knife to my back, possibly kidnapping me.

The blood drains from my face and bile rises in my throat.

Is that what's happening? He's kidnapping me?

I'm going to be sick at any moment. The telltale stomach cramps have already set in.

"That's it," the man says, voice slow and deep—praising? "Keep going. Straight ahead." It's almost like he senses the oncoming nausea. Like he's trying to reduce the immediate threat with soothing words.

It's ridiculous. I know there's nothing safe about those words. They're a twisted illusion.

Yet my stomach settles.

He guides me through the exit and onto the raised parking lot on a large platform. I hear a train pull in below us, screeching on the tracks as it comes to a halt. A woman walks past us with hastened steps—maybe to catch said train—and she doesn't even spare us a glance.

I want to reach out and tug at her, scream for help. But I don't dare. And as the man behind me moves us across the platform, toward the stairs at the corner, help slips out of reach.

I know what's down there beneath the long set of stairs.

Nothing.

The stairs lead to the secluded side of the station, where people only come when the parking space up here is full. And it sure isn't today.

The shaking spreads through my body, and I start staggering.

I abruptly halt at the edge of the stairs and stare down the immense amount of steps. "I can't," I croak. Somehow, it seems worse falling down all those steps than being dragged away by this stranger. "I'll fall."

"*Dershu tebya.* I won't let you fall." As if to prove his point, he tightens his grip on my arm.

It's like déjà vu—the steadying hand and deep voice.

That's when it hits me. The man on the train. White and black. His suit.

I turn my head and stare straight up into chilly blue eyes. Cold as a block of ice, yet warm with the promise he just made. It doesn't make sense—not the dichotomy in his eyes, not the kidnapping.

I'm so stunned my fear fades for a moment, making my feet move on autopilot as he nudges me.

Fresh notes of citrus and something masculine waft past my nose as I move my feet onto the first step, and I inadvertently inhale a deep whiff of the intoxicating scent. *His scent.*

"One step at a time. I'll catch you if you fall."

He must be mocking me for my unsteady feet—or maybe my fall on the platform earlier. But I find no ridicule in his words. They are smooth and warm. Tender even. Maybe he actually means it?

It can't be. How can someone be tender while holding a knife to my back?

My brain fogs over with all the questions and contradictions. Yet somehow, I manage to zero in on the task of placing one foot on each step—a task that seems more like climbing a mountain than a simple everyday action.

I barely notice that the sharp tip at my back disappears and a flat palm presses against my waist instead. Supporting me?

It takes forever to descend those stairs, and when I finally have both feet back on solid ground, it takes me a moment to gather my thoughts. Before I can think of running, the knife is back against my skin. The man leads me to the dusty parking lot in front of the rails, where a single large SUV is parked in the shadow of the platform.

My skin stings beneath the tip of the knife, but the pain is nothing compared to the one bearing down on my chest. I can barely breathe through it, and my inhales become more and more ragged as we approach the car.

The faint noise of traffic hums in the distance, but it's so low I barely notice it. My wheezing breath and the crunch of shoes on gravel seem to be the only sounds around us.

Stopping by the SUV, the man opens the back door, and I see the silhouette of another man in the driver's seat. The driver is large and bulky, like one of those men you see pulling a truck on TV.

Heavy blocks of ice settle in my stomach. I can't get into that car. When I'm in, there's no out. I know it like I know sunsets leave darkness, heavy clouds bring rain. And like the weather, I see no stopping this. Yet my mind scrambles to work something out.

Should I fight? Scream? Is it worth risking a knife in my back?

Indecision pounds in my head, dragging on in a single second that seems to last forever.

Then the last question becomes void as the knife hits the ground with a metallic sound. The sharp tip is gone, and I know what I have to do.

There's no way I'm getting into that car.

With a forceful yank of my arm, I open my mouth to scream. But I'm too slow. Before the shrill sound can ring out into the open space, a large hand clamps over my mouth.

"Don't even think about it." The words are a low snarl, and for a moment, I think it's someone else—maybe the man in the car who has come out. It can't be the same voice as the one crooning in my ear moments ago. "The knife was just a means to keep you calm. But down here, I'm not beyond using force."

It's the same man. The citrusy scent from before wafts past my nose again, and the other man is still in the driver's seat. There's no one else here. The man snarling in my ear is the same one who pressed a supportive hand against my waist and promised he wouldn't let me fall.

Maintaining the punishing grip on my bicep, he removes his palm from my mouth, and what little courage I had gathered fades fast.

There's a rustle of clothes—a hand digging into a pocket. The seconds stretch on, and I don't understand why he doesn't shove me into the vehicle.

Something new drops to the ground. Plastic? I glance down, and yes, there on the gravel lies a small, oblong plastic cap, and somehow, that lid is more terrifying than the knife beside it.

The man pulls down my arm, stretching my shoulder. And then I feel it. The most terrifying thing of all. A small prick, then an aching pressure as liquid seeps into my muscle.

I whimper—a small, weak sound. My body slackens as my strength seeps out with frightening speed. My limbs go numb, and my knees give in. I collapse.

As the man promised, he catches me. Strong arms easily support my weight, holding me against a hard chest.

Using my last sliver of strength, I crane my neck and gaze up into a set of blue eyes boring into my very soul. I don't recognize the features around them, but I recognize the intensity of those eyes.

It *is* him. Aleksandr Pletnev.

"It's you..." My voice fades before I can say more.

"You're mine now." His lips tip up into a wide, charming smile—the smile I so badly wanted on the train. Now, he finally aims it at me, and it's the most terrifying thing I've ever seen.

The last thing I see before my world goes black.

ABOUT ELLA

Ella Jacobs writes dark and kinky romance. Her books all center around Dom/sub dynamics, ranging from BDSM relationships with light dub con to pitch-black captor/captive stories with Stockholm syndrome and heavy non con.

What all her stories have in common is the emotional depth that makes them feel very raw and real. They will pull at all your heartstrings, maybe gut you and shock you, and take you through the emotional wringer.

Ella lives in Northern Europe, where she has been part of the BDSM community for many years. She lives her own age-gap romance with a stern, loving Dominant, who is always ready for some character analysis and rarely gets jealous when she falls in love with her fictional men.

Besides writing, Ella loves to play music and travel.

You can read more about her own experiences with the BDSM lifestyle on her website.

www.ellajacobs.com

ALSO BY ELLA JACOBS

Enslaved Series

Pitch black, captivity, interconnected standalones

Take Me

Break Me

Heal Me

Delivered to the Devil

Raw & emotional, heavy non-con, standalone

His in the Darkness

FREE dark and spicy novella

In His Cage

Abduction, Stockholm Syndrome, standalone

Not Yours Trilogy

Raw & emotional BDSM with dub con

Not Yours to Keep

If I Were Yours

Printed in Dunstable, United Kingdom